Unmailed Letters To a Married Woman

by

Mr. X

Published by

TRAFFORD Publishing
Suite 6E, 2333 Government St.
Victoria, BC, Canada V8T 4P4

"What goes around, comes around."

National Library of Canada Cataloguing in Publication Data

Mr. X, 1938-
    Unmailed letters to a married woman

ISBN 1-55212-930-6

I. Title.
PS3613.I87U55 2001   813.6   C2001-902627-7

TRAFFORD

This book was published *on-demand* in cooperation with Trafford Publishing.
On-demand publishing is a unique process and service of making a book available for retail sale to the public taking advantage of on-demand manufacturing and Internet marketing.
On-demand publishing includes promotions, retail sales, manufacturing, order fulfilment, accounting and collecting royalties on behalf of the author.

Suite 6E, 2333 Government St., Victoria, B.C. V8T 4P4, CANADA
Phone   250-383-6864   Toll-free   1-888-232-4444 (Canada & US)
Fax   250-383-6804   E-mail   sales@trafford.com
Web site   www.trafford.com   TRAFFORD PUBLISHING IS A DIVISION OF TRAFFORD HOLDINGS LTD.
Trafford Catalogue #01-0332   www.trafford.com/robots/01-0332.html

10   9   8   7   6   5   4   3

List of Poems

PROLOGUE

The Romantic pursues the unattainable. Mr. X caught it and attains more than he expected.

Mr. **X** and millions of men have similar stories. If you are not one of them, you probably know somebody who is. Tritely, the story could be called "Romeo and Juliet for Graybeards," with internal rather than external prohibitions to the relationship. Love cares not at what age it strikes

Unmailed Letters shows how love removes limitations; the limitations placed on us by others which we accept and by ourselves. It brings a new sense of power beyond armies, beyond wealth, beyond magic. Its price is the comfort of our limitations.

As Gibran said in The Prophet, "*Though his voice may shatter your dreams as the north wind lays waste the garden. . . . So shall he descend to your roots and shake them in their clinging to the earth.*" Or, as Garth Brooks sings, "God's greatest blessings are unanswered prayers."

DAVID'S CURSE

Tiny
beauty large inside
manifested physically
and I desire her
as David did Bathsheba.

I have no authority
over Uriah's fatal battle
with the White Lady.
He is there
of his own will.

You speak of intimacies
that perhaps
best remain unsaid
for fantasies leap
into my mind.

Extended caresses,
touching, kissing, then
draining
the last sweet drop
of love nourishment
from the depths
of your ecstatic body
while you in turn
are simultaneously enriched
from mine,
and we...

must wait.
1/19/93

10/23/93 5 PM

Dearest Donna,
      Since I have more free time than you, I guess I'll write first. I'll put these in the sock drawer so you can look at them when (if?) you come over. I'm glad we spoke earlier. "Strange" how we were thinking the same thing about not seeing each other until you could get rid of the ugly spot on your ring finger. I'm so glad you thought of letters. I was just going to go for your phone calls. (Speaking of letters, remember the one to your sister.)
      You occupy the center of my mind - sometimes I wish I could think of other things. Wendy, the tiny hostess at California Cafe, has known about you for a few months now. Obviously, because she is tiny, she attracted me, temporarily. It lasted until my second look when I saw her rings. We've become pretty close, her husband is in the car business too. Someday when this is over and beginning, I want to introduce you to her and all my friends so they can see how blessed I am. Anyway, since I'm always thinking of you, it's no wonder you hear me call your name.
      Donna, I'm so scared. For all the women in my life, this is something new and fresh. Loving you is probably the easiest thing I've ever done. Being with you is a glimpse of heaven. Looking in your eyes is like being swallowed by love. And with all this, I'm scared. I guess it's because it's new. I have loved before, always unrequited. Simply practice for when you came along. I have some great poetry from this. First I learned I could love. Then I learned 1000 ways without sex. Then I learned oneness. From you I became aware I could have learned all this from the same woman. Now it's here. Oh shit! What do I do now? Just keep going I guess.
Love,
X

8 PM

Dearest Donna,

Well, I've been sanding down the old kitchen stool. I started the project last year when I was working on the louvers, but I've been pretty tired in the evening this spring and Summer. I heard this was the hottest year in 600 years I have no idea how they came to that conclusion, but I had heat exhaustion twice. Anyway, I figured I better get these projects done while I have time. This is going to be the longest six weeks of my life. Maybe I'll paint the house. I'd better take a shower. It was lead paint I was sanding.

10 PM Arrrg! I had to go get my Chocolate Chip ice cream. Honey, I hate to tell you this, but I think I might be addicted to Chocolate Chip. When I run out of my stash I go bonkers. I'm so sorry, but these are the things you should know about me. Regrettably, I'm not perfect.

I think this is the "dependency phase " of the relationship. I feel dependant on you - just to be. Not to "be there" or "be there for me," but just to be. Your existence, your being is so important to me, just in the fact you are who you are. This is neat! Time to iron. Love you, X

10:30 Just still thinking about you. Only ironed one shirt. Three pants to go.

11:20 Done. A couple of dishes, make the coffee and to bed. It's so nice to have something to look forward to. I wonder if I'll win the $15 million Lotto. Things could move forward more quickly if I did. But then, I would not have the opportunity to support you when you opened the store. Well, I got two of 'em. I'm usually happy if I get one! See how lucky you are for me? Honey, I guess this letter kind of shows you what I've been telling you. You are in my thoughts all the time. This is good snugglin' weather. Wish you were here. I'd like to hold you all night. There I go getting dependent again. Besides, I don't think I'd make it. Oh well. I guess I'll make the coffee and do some dishes and some dreaming.

Love,

X

10/24/93 6:30 AM

Dearest Donna,

I've had my first cup of coffee, and needless to say, I've been thinking about you. I had a wonderful present for you this morning. It's mostly gone now.

It's so strange to me. I know I am a good man and deserve the kind of love you show me. I can feel it when you just look at me, and in your hugs. It is so empowering. And I know at this time there are so many things keeping you from expressing it fully. They will pass. Some, painfully. The pain is mandatory. Suffering is optional and I hope not one you choose.

I usually sit in the darkness waiting the sun while drinking my coffee and smoking too many cigarettes. Writing you, I cut down a little on smoking. This is good. I need to quit. Who knows? Maybe your love will fill the need I keep trying to fill with cigarette smoke. We'll see.

Soon I'll be getting ready for church. The process is: a morning muffin, the comics, editorials, word search and six different things in the comics. Today, the preacher is on the 4th commandment. Next week the fifth. Then Advent and he'll pick up 6 - 10 in January. I think I coveted. I'll look it up in the dictionary. Covet: "To desire inordinately without due regard to the rights of others, desire wrongfully." Inordinate is not within proper limits or excessively. I think we can make a good case for staying in proper limits. Rights have associated with them responsibilities. I believe we have acted responsibly (darn it!) within proper limits. You have more than held your end of the contract, and it is admirable you still do, in spite of our desire. Of course, you are worth waiting for. The clock chimed seven. Time for a paper, shower and muffin.
Love,
X

1:30 PM

Dearest Donna

Second quarter and the Dolphins are killing the Colts. Hooray! I was thinking about you in church this AM, wishing you were there, feeling like you were. I sit 2-4 pews from the back on the left next to the aisle. I sit there to get out quickly to get to the goodies in Fellowship Hall before the other kids. Anyway, I was sitting there, right leg over left knee, just like you were there. I wait for tea water to boil; I'll make a couple of gallons, then get back to sanding.

7 PM

I noticed the hole in my life today. I was hoping your phone call would fill it. You say the most wonderful things to me. They are truly soul food, validating me as I try to validate you

I know that at this time you might feel like a prickly, heavy blanket is draped over you, with the only escape the solace of your bedroom. It would be foolhardy for you to call from there, and you are no fool. I do miss you. You will know when it is exactly right. I'm sure of that.

A couple of very important things: 1. Do you like anchovies on your pizza? If not, it's OK. They know how to make only half with. 2. You will have to pass the Sam/Tiffany test. These are friends who love me very much. From what I have told them about you, they approve, so it is no sweat. After they meet you, they're going to wonder how I got so lucky!

The stool is 3/4 sanded. I can finish it tomorrow after I mow. I broke one of the step supports at the tongue and groove joint. My son will bring me a bar clamp tomorrow and I'll fix it.

Honey, I don't know if all this small stuff is a diversion from the deep love I have for you or an attempt to share other parts of my life with you?

I wait

> *from predawn past midnight*
> *to hear the sound of her voice.*
> *Sweet words from sweeter lips.*
> *The sound of love in her voice*
> *- strange upon my ear.*
> *God's music.*

It comes not, yet

> *I remember the dulcet tones of love*
> *and must dream of memories*
> *as she faces reality.*
> *Angels protect this angel*
> *that she stub not her little toe*

That

> *she is wrapped in the aegis*
> *of God's love, safe.*
> *Amen, and so it is*
> *I can send only snuggling love*
> *to warm her as a comforter*
> *sent from afar.*

Love,

X

10/25

Dearest Donna,

I was so hoping you would call - hoping you got the message from Roberta. Samantha gave me an Idea to get you out of this mess quickly. Actually, they don't have you by the short hair; you have them! Call your fancy lawyer. Tell the receptionist you must speak to him on a new matter. You want a divorce because your husband is a crack addict. You both work at the same place and the boss has threatened to fire you if you leave him. You have four kids and cannot afford to lose your job. Can he help you and can he get Ralph to pay? Later, you can mention to him you have a complete set of books on the shop.

You, my Dearest, are in the catbird seat! You can even get a temporary restraining order tailored not to affect Ralph's job duties. Wow!

You know, I don't think either of us ever believed this kind of powerfully gentle and passionate love was available; that it even existed, except in romance novels, and we are both holding back! When we stop holding back, do you think the alarms from Turkey Creek nuclear power plant will go off? This might be embarrassing, but who cares?

10/26 5:30 AM

Dearest Donna

I've been up since 4, thinking about you, worrying about you, just trying to send my love to you, asking for your protection. I hope you can contact the fancy lawyer - and I haven't even told you yet - and something can be done to get you free. Your words, "I am coming to you" bounce around in my heart and bring me great joy. Yet, right now, I would sacrifice them for your freedom. You are too wonderful and deserving a person to be in this trap.

There are five different Greek words for love. Though I have a lot of *eros*, I guess there is some *agape* there for you also. Flash! Maybe *agape* is the magic ingredient in the mix? I don't know. Maybe it is *philos* rather than *agape*. Maybe both. I've never been here before so I'm having a little trouble with identification. I don't know if it makes any difference, except perhaps for others.

I look forward to your freedom, wanting to spend time with you. We agree on so much conceptually, yet we have not had the opportunity to put these things into practice. There are so many things, for all our openness with each other, we just don't know. Boy, do I want to find out! I'll bet you didn't know I liked CC ice cream, and I have no idea exactly what your tastes are - in food that is. At least you're an "outie." And of course there are times when your radiance so blinds me; I could care less which

way you hang the T.P. I look forward to both learning from and more about you.
Love,
X
P.S. When are we going to fight about something? It means we've entered the counter-dependent phase of relationship and full interdependency will be near. Wow! Of course, I'm not rushing things. (Ho. Ho.) - **X**

6 PM+
      We spoke today - too briefly. When I cannot be with you, I will settle for talking with you. When I cannot talk with you, I love to listen to your messages. I ate very little yesterday. Maybe if I eat a lot tonight, I'll sleep better. Of course, were you here instead of there, I would be sleeping the sleep of the satiated, like a hungry lion who just devoured a young gazelle. Damn! I miss you! More later.
X

8 PM
      Well, I had another Steak salad - feel better, and as always, thinking of you. I hope your memories of Friday are as succulent as mine. The memories of my fantasy - you snuggling in the chair with me - were tough to live with. The memories of that reality - you snuggling with me and the pure joy I felt with you in my arms - Oh precious one. What your presence in my life does for me! Even those brief moments, were so special. Hell, you probably had to block them. Did you know as I bend to kiss you, your lips swell with passion, engorged with desire? You can't block that.
      I guess this is a part of my problem. These moments of tenderness are to be shared. I share them back with you on paper, yet you are not there to receive them. I can shout, "I love you" here, and you cannot hear me, there. As I write, I cannot share these words with you. At least they are out of me and somewhere where eventually you can see or hear them.

I went over to X Jr.'s and told them (Tanya too) I might have a girlfriend soon. This will happen when you un-block, and for your own safety, you can't, yet. What a pain in the ass this is! Anyway, I found out I hid the bar clamp from myself, so I'll clamp the step leg tomorrow.

I now begin page 9. Damn! I'm really getting prolific! Thinking of you, words run headlong from my heart through my arm and pen onto this paper. A wondrous experience. On the other hand, were you here, I doubt if I would be writing, so every circumstance has its positive side. Oh. Have you got the message yet? I'll stop so you can answer me with a yes or no. If yes, what is the message? I love you? Whatever gave you that idea? I must stop this. I'm going to see what is on the tube and go to bed. It's been a long day.

Love,

X

10/27 6 AM

Dearest Donna,

The nicest part of sitting in the morning darkness is knowing the sun will rise. And I wait for you as I await the sunrise. I must admit, the sun is quicker - more regular than you, but it is not human. It can only warm my days, but you can warm my nights in a way the sun never dreamt.

So, here we are again, together in our separateness. Fearful, longing, living a half-life growing shorter and longer at the same time. For the moment, I smile outside myself, looking at me and you and us; three separate entities, the latter having the most importance in my life.

The laundry churns, approaching spin dry. Wednesday is sheet day and they will be clean and freshly talcumed tonight. This weekend - first of the month - is the rest of the bedding; pad, pillows and spread. It's just a habit from living alone. Into the dryer and soon my work day will begin.

Well, my Dearest, I have other letters to write, I will close with you, as always in my thoughts.

Love,

X

ENOUGH

As I caressed her face
she trembled...
anticipating resolution
to conflict within.
Resolution we knew
would not come
today.

Her eyes teared
with powerful new emotion
and my new kissed finger
touched her lips, comforting
as a hug.

"Intimacy,"
she whispered surprised,
trembling again
while my fingers grazed
softly on her arms.

My gentle kiss
as one anticlimactic
in the afterglow
simply said...

enough.

5:45 PM

Dearest Donna,

I love your name! Anyway, I had the feeling today when I was reading you the first 10 pages, you were selectively tuning out - a self defense mechanism I use at poetry when the subject matter is too intense. Overall, you got the message and that is important, so if you were tuning out the intense stuff, I can neither complain nor criticize when I do it myself.

I hope you have a little understanding of how much I respect this aspect of your behavior. We know what is between us, and I know how much work it is for you to stay focused on where you are. Lady, you are great! You see, I figure eventually you will understand the rules and consequences of The Game you are playing. Player 1 is the addict/abuser/manipulator. Player 2 is the co-dependent/abusee/manipulator.

Player 1: (Takes some adverse action on Player 2)

Player 2: (Withdrawal, rejection)

Player 1: "I promise I won't do it again."

Player 2: "We'll see." (Guarded.)

Player 1: (Behaves, as Player 2 lowers their guard, then Bammo, Socko!)

Player 2: (Withdrawal, rejection.)

Player 1: "I promise I won't do it again. I'll cut back. (With sincerity, because they   actually believe it.) "I'll do anything you want me to."

Player 2: "Go to_______. (A.A., C.A., N.A., Church, spiritual guide, guru, etc.)

Player 1: "O.K. Honey. I'll do anything for you." (Goes, behavior improves, Player 2 lowers guard; Bammo, Socko!)

Player 2: (Withdrawal, rejection)

The Game is played in millions of homes all over this country and I'm sure many people have different names for it. It establishes a behavior pattern where Player 2 offers hope to Player 1. Player 1 wins The Game because hope is all they need. Player 2 also wins because the behavior pattern stays the same and they are doing the "right thing" by offering hope and keeping some for themselves.

The truth is, both lose. Until Player 1 is utterly hopeless, there is no hope. Player 2 dies, either inside or literally. Even

the process sucks. Maybe now you know why I worry. I wrote
this script a long time ago, me and a few others. Ralph and
millions others just happen to be borrowing it. Yes, I believe in
miracles. I have to. I am one and my next breath proves it. I
just have never seen on with crack.

Now, precious one, forget about me, about us. Think
only for a while about the wonderful, beautiful, loving person
God put on this earth to love and be loved and mother the fine
children you have raised. I know Ralph has great qualities. You
would not have married him if he didn't. But let me ask you, if
you knew then what you know now - he and his former wife
smoked crack so they could get it on - would you have married
him? I didn't think so. From a legal standpoint, this is called a
lack of full disclosure on a material matter. It can be construed
as fraud in the making of the contract. It's almost as if he didn't
tell you about another wife he had stashed somewhere.

Donna, you know I love and want you, but more than
this, I want you to be free. At least free from this destructive
game. That must be a first priority. I don't ever want to play it
again with anybody. It gives me the creeps to see it played by
people I love, no matter how I love them. Another thing, to me
you ARE the ultimate, living, loving aphrodisiac. If he can't see
that, he doesn't deserve you.

I also know - or at least have heard - people in Hell want
ice water. So what I want can be of no value to anyone else. It is
simply my want. I also want for you your highest good. I want
to see God's JOY in your life, not mere happiness. (Happiness
comes for Player 2 when Player 1 temporarily does what Player
2 asks.) In my experience no one's highest good comes from The
Game. Now you know the rules of The Game, the futility of
playing The Game, and the Final Outcome of The Game. Your
choice.

Donna, let me tell you about Mary, the mother of my
children. Two years after our divorce, she remarried a short,
dark, ex-Marine who was working as a jailer. Of course I am
tall, blonde, and IV-F. I guess with booze, I was Mary's "jailer."
One day, Sarah called and asked, "Daddy, watcha watchin' on
TV?" I said "Startrek" and she said, "Oh well, Bob is watching
that here and I wanted to watch something else." Maybe Bob

and I weren't so different after all. After I got sober, I could not hide my shame as well and I lost a lot of my arrogant self-righteousness. This and other things, I'll tell you about later, if you are interested, just blew whatever illusion we held about each other. She and Bob seem to be happy in Ohio.

Donna, I said I wrote the script. True and not true. Every one of us drunks and addicts (regardless of the particular addiction) write pretty much the same script for ourselves. As I reread what I wrote, it sounded quite arrogant. I think you know what I meant, I just didn't like how it sounded.

Listen, little Miss Perfect, (for me anyway), Miss Human Being, Miss Wonderful, I love you. I miss you. I want to give you things; at this time they would be totally inappropriate, like flowers and stuff. All I have to offer is me, patiently waiting for you.

Love,

X

10/28/93 6:30 AM

Dearest Donna,

I've thought a lot about what I wrote last night. Your choice is not between Ralph and X, it is between life and death. I understand the commitment to marriage and I love you for it. Honey, I think the Holy Roman Catholic Church would give you an annulment in a heartbeat under these circumstances. I know about feelings and love and being torn apart emotionally, and I hurt for you too. I pray for strength for you to do what is in your best interest. Rilke said life and death are mankind's two greatest gifts, both usually passing unopened. I would beg you to open the gift of life.

Love,

X

7 PM

Honey, I just got home and listened to your message and am a little confused. I thought you were seeing a lawyer about divorce, about keeping your job, etc. or was Ruth there? Well, I thought about you a lot, and talked about you a little, and found myself very angry - at myself of course. I understand Ralph very well. I know the fear of losing you, not as a friend, but as one with whom I am considering - Hell! Dreaming about - sharing the rest of my life. Before last Friday, my fantasies were little and now they are realized. Now they are bigger and seem to be snatched away.

A week ago Tue., I started grieving the loss of my fantasies. It wasn't bad. They were small but highly valued. Then you fulfilled them. You sat in the chair with me. I showed you a bonding exercise. Just what I dreamed about. How wonderful it was. Now, I don't know where the hell I am and think you are in the up phase of The Game as Player 2.

I'll call you in the morning - maybe write more tonight. I'm hungry now.

Love,

X

Where am I?
Where do I stand?
May I hold you in my arms?
Take your hand?

I am your friend
But lover too
I don't know.
Tell me, do you?

10/29 11:58 PM

Dearest Donna,

I just made it home before my coach turned into a pumpkin, or whatever it is supposed to do. I was over at Tiffany's earlier. She wanted me to meet her new boyfriend - and of course my topic of conversation was you, and our "status." Then I went to get something to eat and go hunting. Tiffany recommended Il Gardino.

You see, precious one, I listened to you today and I heard what you said You weren't aware of it - I don't think -but I listened. In talking about the appointment with the preacher tonight, you said, "we are going . . . " You and Ralph are still a "we." Had you said "Ralph and I," well that has an entirely different connotation.

So my Dearest, you are not consciously aware of it yet, but you are staying where you are. There is no logic to this. There never is where drugs are involved. I could say, "I don't understand . . .," but I don't have to. I could point out the things you have told me: you want me and love me as you have never loved and wanted before; you think I am the greatest lover you have ever known and we haven't done anything yet; and the half hour we spent together a week ago that left you shaking was the happiest you had been in a long time. I know you meant all of these things yet, they seem to mean very little in reality. The reality appears to be you and Ralph have won The Game. So, I went hunting.

I ran into Tiffany, her sister and mom at Il Gardino. I had been looking. Tiffany asked if I saw any one I liked. I simply told her there was nothing there as fine as what I was leaving. You are a tough act to follow!

What I sense right now is you are caught in an emotional entanglement more powerful than our love. Our love is the most powerful I have ever felt, so I have no choice but to surrender. I love you as I have never loved before. Then again, until about eight years ago, I didn't know I could love or what it was and I guess I am still a child in this field. And my Dearest, from behind your walls, I know you love me too: deeply, powerfully, and passionately. You can say you love the Lord in me or you

love the spirit of Christ in me or however you need to put it for
your protection, but it is there as sure as sunrise. I also know you
never loved Ralph like this, yet you will stay in a morally invalid
marriage anyway. Oh, it is legally valid. There were no
misstatements of fact on the legal application for the license.
Yet, you said if you knew then what you know now, absolutely
not. Go figure?

It may have been true what Ralph says about your sister,
but she is not his pusher. He was doing drugs long before he met
her or you. Blaming her makes a good excuse for his behavior, I
think this is a diversion. It will happen again and again and
again. And you will stay without reason, like millions of other
women. Ever so slowly the light in your eyes, which is the
beauty of your soul, will begin to dim. I am deeply saddened for
this loss to the world and to me.

Pardon my pessimism. I have seen too much of this. I
ask only God be with you and protect you, because I am selfish
and I love you very much.

Love,

X

10/30 6:30 PM

Dearest Donna,

I want to let you know I will be around for a while - I
dreamt I was in Louisiana last night. Had I met someone last
night at Il Gardino, it would still take a couple of years for me to
trust them enough to give them my heart. Look at you and I've
known how special you are for a long time. Besides, you still
have it.

You may feel a little guilty. Go ahead. It is just as silly
as your staying with Ralph. In my mind and heart, I am the
guilty one. You are simply special. That is the way God made
you, and there is no cause to feel guilt or shame for being a
wonderful child of God. I am the one who erred in allowing

myself to fall in love with a married woman. Perhaps, in time, I
can return to the simple admiration I felt for you for the first
couple of years I knew you. I hope so. You are too special a
person to not have in my life as a friend.
Love,
X
P.S. My dear friends Tiffany, Sam, and Anne, my son and
daughter all say "I love you" to me. In the first person. You are
the only one who says, "You are loved" in the second person. I
really don't like it. I am a first person, not a second! - X

10 PM
Dearest Donna,
        I am saddened for both of us. I feel very powerless right
now. I see the trap you are in and can do no more than offer my
hand to you. I have and you prefer the trap. No, I don't think
you prefer it; more so you believe there is another way out.
There isn't. At least not in my experience.
        Precious one, I do not want to steal your hope as mine
has been self-stolen, for it will sadden you beyond tears. Yet it
will be stolen from you. I do not have the courage to be your
thief. Someday you will see the ups and downs of your
relationship with Ralph are leading down rather than up. It is the
realization I came to with my children's mother, and I didn't
know anything, except what was, wasn't supposed to be.
        You have given me a very bright spot in my life. When I
am down in the dumps - as now - the thought of my children
always cheers me up. Now I have two children and the thought
you love me - even though you won't act on it. I have never felt
anything ever from anyone the way I felt your love and you were
holding back! Donna Dearest, in my life, that is the way it is
supposed to be, a gentle super power. Were you ever to touch
me in love without holding back, that power would bring tears of
joy to my eyes, shivers and goose bumps.
Love,
X

MAN'S FALL

I sit in the shadow of sadness
Its cloak folded over my form.
Knowing the value of my loss;
Her body to keep me warm.

Her soul snow white with freckles
The very same color as mine.
Her heart so warm with giving love
Her features delicately fine.

I felt the power of oneness
A promise of things to come.
And the shadow now destroys it.
As though I am on the run.

I run into my hiding place
To privately lick my wound
A long sharp knife thrust deep within
Twisted in the light of the moon.

The loss I feel is buried deep
I know not if it is real.
The words she says unknowing
Unearth the pain I feel.

Her words of love are shielded
Guarded, as if they might kill.
I know they exist, my heart pounds not;
The beat grows evermore still.

At last I lay in silence
The dead wind blows no sound.
The inky blackness covers life,
All becomes the grave digger's mound.

And so I sit and ponder
Any value in the giving.
Some others gratefully take them
So I guess I'll go on living.

A long time coming for stillbirth.
A long time to give her trust.
A long time building to nothing
A long time feeling it just.

But in the time I knew her
Did I know her any at all?
God help me please, I love her, yet
There's no protection from the fall.

10/31/93

11/1/93

Dearest Donna,

I read something saying, "Pain means one is in error." Oops! Boy, am I in error. Loving you is the easiest thing I have ever done. It's even better than Chocolate Chip ice cream! So, what happened in me to cause this pain and darkness? Simple. My expectations and then the expectation of loss of my expectations. Expectation of loss is fear. The only thing I can lose is an expectation. Pooof! It is gone.

There are basically two kinds of expectations; Realistic and Unrealistic. My expectations had the appearance or illusion of being realistic, but in fact were not. I expected you to divorce him, expected me to court you, and I expected to marry you. Those are a lot of expectations to put on a woman who is deeply committed to the institution of marriage and is still married! I apologize for it taking me so long to recognize my error. I think I'll just go back to loving you freely, without all those damn expectations.

What did it was seeing you today in those white shorts and broad striped top and not being able to go up to you and say,"Hi," or get a hug or something. That was painful. The reading and click. I began to understand where I had been in error.

Love is giving freely. When I give with these expectations, it is not really love. I must ask your forgiveness. The love, respect -even admiration - I have felt from you is too precious a memory to me - perhaps still a reality - for me to sacrifice in any way. You want to hear another stupid expectation? I was expecting some sort of commitment from you. How can I when your commitment to the institution is so strong?

Donna, Dearest precious one, this is what happens when I was thinking about you all the time. I didn't stop to look at me. Boy, I need this! It's a quarter to 5. I hope you felt my sigh of relief. It's nice to be human and screw up and figure out where and how. But, I might do it again. I am nuts you know.

Anyway, I released my expectations so I can do the easy stuff - loving you. It's free. You owe nothing for it. You deserve it. It makes me far more joyful this way to love and support you anyway I can, than doing it with expectations. Also, this way I can let life surprise me.

I think this is what is meant by being responsible for my own feelings. I never knew there was so much inner freedom in being responsible. Now, see what you did? If it hadn't been for you, I would not have learned this lesson today. Thank you. Besides, I'd rather desire you than my expectations of you.
Love,
X

11/1/93 9:15 PM

Dearest Donna,

I feel all warm and snugly inside. And this is a hell of a lot better than how I felt around noon today. Loving you this way is a lot more fun. I guess it has a lot to do with faith too. I was telling Anne about you - she runs a dating service - and she said I'd have to go through a thousand women to find another like you. At least! But it's OK. You see, I decided to let The Boss do the picking for me. Don't get me wrong, I sure hope he picks you. But it's out of my hands now. And I can just love you and be very happy. (Another sigh of relief.)

I was sitting here with my thumb in my butt trying to remember what I was going to say. I remembered. It's like we agreed on; what goes around comes around. All I have to do is love, and it will come back. Of course I want it to come back from you, but The Boss decides on how it comes back. When I put the expectations on you, then I am too locked up to see what is happening. This also makes me a pee poor friend. Another very precious thing to me.

The bottom line here is, don't worry about hurting me. You can't. I can. I did. I'm not gonna any more, because it's too much fun this way. So there!
I love you.
X

11/6/93

Dearest Donna,

I know you must keep your focus now. I called last Thursday to wish you the best in the minister meeting. It is so difficult, but necessary. As the saying goes, "a girl's gotta do what a girl's gotta do." Your loyalty is awesome! I will have to warn you about the possible consequences, but it is still awesome.

You know, I was telling Sam about this and mentioned in passing sometimes I can be a jerk. She agreed. Boy, I look forward to someone with such a deep loyalty!

Honey, sometime before the end of the month, I expect it to hit the fan. I'll be here for you.

I love you,

X

11/8/93

Dearest Donna

It was so wonderful to talk with you yesterday. My spirits - among other things - are once again raised. I'm so glad you have something, our love, to smile about.

I want to tell you I think what you are doing in terms of your commitment to the relationship is awesome! As much as I would hate to see you hurt again, I know it will happen. The sooner the better. Time becomes your enemy as his rage builds. I am sure you have asked yourself these questions, but I would like to ask them also, not only so you can answer them to me, but to you.

1. Knowing what you now know, can you fully honor the relationship for the rest of your life? Assume a less than 1% probability his problems will be cured.

2. Consider the key words, "fully honor," is this what The Boss would have you do? There are millions of marriages not fully honored seeming to work all right. I know I want more for myself and I think you do too.

3. If, because of the fraud perpetrated on you, you cannot honor the relationship to the degree you expect from yourself, and the degree you may believe expected from The Boss, what is your best course of action?

4. Any relationship requires work and pain, as we struggle, clinging to old destructive ideas and ideals that must be wrenched from us - sometimes as painful as a live flaying - for we wear these ego colored ideas as a second skin. So how much should we endure and for how long? (My answer comes from the book of Job.) Job endured much while his friends told him

he must have done something wrong for God to treat him this way. Job kept the faith, knowing he had not erred, and was rewarded with a new family, riches and the whole nine yards.

5. You question my respect for you. For me to respect you all you have to do is behave in accordance with what your guts tell you, most of the time. Unfortunately, only one of us ever came close to the fantasied ideals most of us hold as "perfection." So I don't expect you to be perfect, except as the perfect Donna. You are, so that ends that. I expect me to be the perfect X, which means I am oblivious to the obvious on occasion, a jerk in other words. Remember it was Roberta who pointed out to me how much you loved me. She took one look and told me as we left the store, "**X**, that girl really loves you!" Honey, I knew you liked me a lot, loved me - as a friend, even maybe lusted after my bones a little, but loved? I was oblivious to the obvious. Maybe part of me - old tapes - were saying, "a woman of this stature, and beauty and depth and courage and character would not truly love you." I know what I feel all over for you, and were you free to do so, I think you would allow yourself the same joy I feel by loving you. I told you I'm not going to settle for mere happiness. I want the best life has to offer me. You.

You just called again, and I am so grateful. I have not called you since Last Thurs. to wish you well. Unless there is a dire emergency I won't. I know you want to keep your focus. You know I want you to be free to feel what you feel I love to hear from you. I can't help thinking sometimes by trying to express how much I love you, I'm interfering with your focus. Yet, you are worth fighting for. I just want to be careful about your second thoughts. By the way, if you ever seduce me, will you respect me afterwards?

Oh precious one, when it is to be, I see a lot of fun in terms of our laughing with each other about ourselves. Sometimes I think God created man simply to bring humor into His life.

Damn! I forgot to tell you! I told my son and daughter about you too. I told X Jr. shortly after we met George in the store. I tell them, "I'm about to get a girlfriend, after she leaves the joker she's married to. Then I plan to court her for a while."

I don't know . . . maybe it's something in my voice giving me away . . . but those who know me and love me anyway are very happy for me to be the way I am now, whatever that is. I guess that's why I'm a lousy liar. Too easy to read. (P.S. I don't play poker.)

A couple of other things and I can close. Hell! I can only remember one. Like I told you, I'm somewhat of a jerk in some areas, so, when (and if) we get together, and I'm in the process of courting you, I'm liable to enjoy it so much, I'll forget why I'm doing it. On top of which, I probably won't recognize when you are sufficiently healed. As a favor to me, would you please let me know when it's OK for me to ask you to marry me. You can say something like, "Honey, you know the little thing you wanted me to remind you about, well it's time." Then I'll say something like, "Oh Honey, I'm so sorry I forgot to take the garbage out. I'll do it right now." Now you pick up your 2x4 and give me a gentle nudge. That's No. 1 favor.

Number two favor is do you deliver? I need a gallon of paint for my driveway. I have *Courtin' and Sportin'* printed out as a tip if you do. You're definitely one for Courtin'. I'll probably read it Wed. night. You should come by and bring Rhonda.

I love you,
X

11/8/93 (still) 9:30 PM
Dearest Donna,

I feel so warm and snugly inside. The news you gave me today sent my spirits into high orbit. My friends Bob and Ray laugh at me - or with me. Tiffany has such good vibes about this, Sam is telling me to go for it, and Anne repeats herself with you are one in a thousand. I wonder if people know my feet don't touch the ground when I walk.

I want so much them to meet you. They deserve to meet this woman who has brought so much joy into my life. They love me and by proxy, they love you too. This, My Queen, is part of what I meant by sharing you with the world.

Oh teach me to dance, this dance of life
And we shall whirl gracefully o'er the floor.
A pas de deux, plie', leap, twice, click, then land
Yourself in my loving arms, evermore, evermore.

Where does this stuff come from? Do you realize with
you drawing this stuff out of me I can become a great romantic
poet? Look what you do for me. How can I help but love you?
I have this vision of you, wearing only your beautiful
long hair. Clean, radiant or glowing - I'm not sure which is the
better word - standing there waiting my touch, while I stand
motionless, awestruck by the beauty before me. There is no play
here; it is serious, sacred, respected and revered. Then slowly I
caress your face and neck and arms; absorbing your beauty with
my lips and fingertips as I absorbed it with my eyes. I could go
on, but I would rather go on with you.
Love,
X

I have to go on. Donna, I don't think you have ever been
loved like this before. You are such a wonderful, loving person
and deserved to be loved. For as much as I know, I know so
little. Be patient with me as we learn together. I want to grow
with you: grow up, grow old, grow in my ability to love you. It
gives me much pleasure to love you. Being loved by you is
ecstasy, and I haven't felt all of it yet . . . well, I kind of feel it.
(You won't scare me will you?) Oh Honey! Finally, I'm
speechless.
Love,
X

11/9/93

Dearest Donna
A question I must ask, although I know the answer, are
you leaving him for you or me? I think I know you well enough
to know you are doing this for you. I make no difference in this
course of action. Yes, my darling one, it is true I want you - I

think now you are the best part of my life. Yet I too can have feelings of guilt, and my feelings would interfere with us the same way yours would. So far, I believe we have done everything right and I want to keep it this way. "Us," "we," and "our" are the three most important words in relationship. "I love you" is powerful, but compare it to "we love each other." We must always protect the "we," "us," and "our." Until we can say it, I will say,
I love you.
X
11/9/93 5:55 PM

Dearest Donna,

I stopped by the house three times today to see if you had left me a message. I'm totally insane of course. When I turned the corner at 5:50, I looked for your car in my carport and you are still at work! I don't fully know what you feel for me, the way you know how I feel about you. I allow me to express these feelings. You will not allow yourself this pleasure, yet. I think I know, and from all indications, you and your love are the most wonderful things in my life. This is better than my kids and they are the greatest! So I have to live where each moment is an eternity, waiting on the sound of your voice until this is over. My Dearest, Dearest Donna. You are worth the wait. Were each of these eternal moments spent in Hell, you would be worth the wait. (They are not, because I know you are there.)

Honey, I have never felt love from anybody the way I feel it from you. But let me stop and say 15 years ago I was incapable of feeling. I am a babe here, and where ever "here" is, it is wonderful. So, thank you for your love. I shall honor it and treasure it, and return it in better condition than I found it.

I have the feeling when you give your love, you don't hold back a darn thing. Right now you have a dam up to hold it back. But the dam is cracking and I occasionally feel a brief squirt in which I try to bathe. When the dam breaks, I shall be swept away in ecstasy.
Love,
X

COURTIN' AN' SPORTIN'

There's gals for courtin' an' gals for sportin'
An' courtin' sometimes more fun.
One thing about sportin', rather than courtin',
Y'always know when you are done.

Now gals for courtin', not gals for sportin'
Take flowers, that kind of stuff.
Now gals for sportin', not gals for courtin'
They know when to say,"enough."

Now gals for sportin', not gals for courtin'
There's a trouble they do bring.
Between courtin' an' sportin' th' trouble's in sortin'
Which one is doin' which thing.

Well, the other or one, though both can be fun
Courtin' and sportin' are twain.
Mixin' courtin' an' sportin' leaves things importan'
Ya fergit which one is main.

So if ya're courtin', fergit about sportin'
Remember, courtin's more fun.
One thing about courtin', rather than sportin',
You are never, never done.

11/10/93 3:30 AM

Dearest Donna,

I was exhausted last night and crashed shortly after 8. I woke up missing you and thinking about you. This is a terribly wonderful experience: terrible because you are not with me, wonderful because you are.

For all our years, I feel as though we are but small children. I want to say, "I remember teaching my sister to walk," but we don't teach them; we just happen to be there when they are ready. Anyway, I did what my parents did and extended my index fingers for her to grab. She would take a couple of steps and plop down for a while, then repeat the process until she walked unassisted.

Hearing from you gives me the same joy as watching a babe's first steps, magnified a thousand fold. Then I wait until the babe is ready to try again.

It's almost 6 and the second load of laundry is in. I wrote of my heroine. What strength and courage you have! And at the same time, you are so frail and delicate and glow with such beauty. I sigh. I love your humanness, and your willingness to be human. I was so tickled by your thoughts of premarital celibacy and then your awareness of who we are. Your thoughts were identical to mine, regardless of propriety. The fact we are on the same wave length is joyous. A kindred spirit. A soul match. Ah, time and patience. What keeps me going is the joy I receive from my dreams of being with you.
I love you.
X

THE NINTH LION

My heroine descended into
the pit with eight lean lions
to battle them as their teeth
and claws gnashed at her loveliness.

Four were white seductresses
armored impenetrable wisps
of smoke that stole man's soul
while racking and destroying his body.

Four were red rage maned
whose glaring eyes saw naught
as they ripped themselves each other
and whoever into bloody flesh pieces.

All attacked in random concert
strategically withdrawing to lure
her into the tooth claw shredder
again and again and again and again.

Slowly sorrowfully she ascended
from Hell's depths to safety while
crept in the ninth lion of death
devouring all there as they themselves.

7:30 AM
Dearest Donna,

I must soon hook up the trailer, but I have an idea I want to share with you. We both know we will not wait for our first time. Our hunger is great. So let us do as much as we can to make it as right as we possibly can by washing each other in the shower before. A simple symbolic gesture of washing away our past so we may come together before God as clean as we can possibly be. I so want our first time to be the fullest at emotional, spiritual and physical levels. We shall shoot for the stars and grow from there.
Love,
X

Noon
Dearest Donna,

I just finished a couple of PB&J sandwiches and hope to get a nap. You would have laughed at me this morning - or with me. I drove off to go to work and forgot to hook up the trailer. It seems my mind is elsewhere. I sent you a kiss over the phone this morning, hoping you would return it with a call.

Donna, I've never gone this far out on a limb before. I'm a little - no, a lot scared. I'm in love with a married woman. One whose feelings have changed toward her husband because she found out who he is. One who has dammed up her feelings for me so she can survive for a short while longer in her present circumstances. One whom I love very much.
X

6:30 PM
Dearest Donna,

And there I fell asleep for an hour or so. After shaking awake, I went for a glass of tea at The Ale House to give Sandy a hard time and tell her about you, and what a miracle it is you are in my life to the extent you are. Sandy is a surrogate daughter - she was a mint guard at Padrino's. You know, one of those girls at the register who keep you from stealing too many mints. I go to Padrino's for Wed.'s offering of black beans and rice. Tonight is poetry and I will be able to share a little of you, maybe with a small part of the world.

Donna, I so want to elevate you consciously to the status of "beloved." You are, of course, I just want to be able to say it to you and introduce you to my friends as "my beloved" and jump up and down and click my heels instead of this interminable waiting. A phone call message to let me know you still smile, you are OK and hanging in. Anything! I think it would be better were one of us in Denver or Boise or Botsuwalla, Zaire. I will survive. You will survive. We will survive, 'till we can live.
Love,
X

11 PM
Dearest Donna,

I'm going nuts. Don't worry, it's not far. Never has been. Please say something to me. I'm sorry to be so weak. So insecure. It's my fault. I <u>know</u> you must avoid showing anything and this is just as hard on you as me. Why are we so damn hard on ourselves?

I must have asked for - and received - four hugs from Ginny (she needs them as badly as I; only 19 and lost a child to SIDS) one from Mable and one from MaryAnne - they're both married. Honey, it just ain't the same. I miss you terribly. I can't talk to you. You can't talk to me. If you do, it will show. By the way, how dumb do you think Ruth is? My kids knew I was getting a divorce before I did. But I'm not too swift.

I will, you will survive, until we can live.
I love you.
X

11/11 7 AM

Dearest Donna,
    I have to shut down. Maintain denial. Deny my feelings. Forget. This is simply a protective device, as you have done. Somewhere, I am still here. I need you and you cannot be here. If you call, you the break your shutdown. What a stupid situation! I regret I have no other alternative but I will lose what little sanity I have if I do not. Forgive me.
X
7 PM
Dearest Donna,
    I did very well today. Only checked the answering machine five times till I got home at 6:30. Intellectually, I completely understand what is going on and all the possible "why's." You have the motivation, with the kids, with him, to remain shut down. You are relying on your own strength, and the Boss's, to get you through this. I think you feel if we talk, it will show, you will start to feel and weaken you. Intellectually, I understand. Emotionally, this sucks!
    I don't sleep. I'm getting sick. My tooth aches. I'm tired. I'm anxious. I'm down. (This is the first of these the psychic predicted, so I'm glad it's here. Two more to go.) Damn! Were it we were not in love with each other! I will consciously not feel it. (I'm so damn funny.) Oh well. Write when you get news.
X

11/13 - 5:30 AM

Dearest Donna,
    Well having a wisdom tooth pulled and having some skinny little gal wanting to jump my bones does a lot to help me de-focus off you. Unfortunately, you are a lot more fun to focus on. It was kind of like popping a boil. All the insanity just whooshed away. Now my dear, I can just wait for your call more calmly, to see what is going on. Maybe this is why vanGogh cut off his ear?

Anyway, my Dearest, you know and I know how well we compliment each others lives. You know and I know how our values and needs blend so perfectly. I think it is silly to waste such an opportunity, but we humans are pretty silly critters sometimes. I'm sure God created us to bring laughter into the universe.

I love you.

X

11/14/93 4:40 PM

Dearest Donna,

Sam is still out; the soup is yet to be eaten. Talking with you brings near orgasmic relief. You are so wonderful. Oh precious one, I needed your reassurance. Thank you one thousand times over. The limb I'm on is a lot thicker now.

Good idea, praying. One of the reasons I need you is I keep forgetting about the neat stuff. You have the ability to remind me at exactly the right time. I love you. Were I to say it a million times, it would not completely express it. Thanks for being in my life. (Sam's here.) I love you.

X

10 PM

Dearest Donna,

Sam's gone - leaving me with the dishes. She had to get to rehearsal. Oh well, no biggie. I'd do the same for Sarah. I know you're lousy with names. Sarah's my daughter.

Sam was talking about some potential problems with her boyfriend's mother. I explained in simple graphic terms what I believe the marriage commitment is all about. It's very simple: we must cleave from all others. Were we married and you and Sarah were drowning, I would get you first. (I'd try and get both of you, but if I couldn't, you would come first.) This is not because I'm so in love with you I'm crazy, it's also about the vows we will have taken. Sarah and X Jr. were gifts from God. I don't know what I did to deserve them - or you for that matter - but they are precious gifts. The vows I took with their mother, I then had no concept of. Unfortunately, the Law doesn't really give a damn about what I am or am not aware of. I paid. Now I know better. You come first. I'd probably do it now, but . . . I'm nuts.

When I told Sam, it took her back a piece. I just told her in my view it was the best representation of the marriage vows I could give her. It's serious stuff. Not to be trifled with. I also told her if my son-in-law and I were drowning, Sarah had better pick him, or I'd spank her!

Now my Dearest one, consider where you are and he and I are drowning. To which of us are you married? Other than implied through thought, word, and our too brief hugs, we have yet to formally take the vows. The vows you gave him were based on deceit. Please my Dearest, I am fighting as hard as I can for you. You have given me your trust because I have been honest with you. In this battle, I don't know if I trust me. So, please ask somebody - maybe a minister, priest or rabbi who is a stranger about the moral validity of your vows.

I really have very little faith in man's laws, it's God's I am concerned with. I cannot pretend to either know them all or pretend to spout them when I am so deeply involved at an emotional level. Most important to me is I don't want to betray your trust in me. I need to tell you, what I'm telling you could be far out in left field. I love you so much, and I'm scared I might be confusing love with desire and I do desire you so much but I love you more. So, ask somebody, will ya?

I am sorry, precious one, for all of my apparent maturity, strength and wisdom, part of me is still an insecure child. I know it and can admit it. That's the first step. The second is, "Came to believe no human power could relieve . . . " this difficulty. Honey, you are only a human power, and one of the things I love about you is you keep reminding me about the Boss.

Roberta was telling me Bob had to wait eight years for her to leave an abusive marriage. Yes, I love you that much, but Bob was a much younger man.

Beyond my desire, I do not like seeing you torn, yet I am aiding and abetting in this ripping. I know it is painful. The pain is mandatory. Suffering is optional. You have been suffering. The pain is cheaper.

I'd better do the dishes and put what's left of the soup in the freezer. Sam really had an appetite tonight! It's nothing compared to my appetite for you. (I'M STARVING!)

By the way, you held and hold the key to my lock down, shut down turned offedness. When you said "I love you," I melted like warm butter in a hot skillet. I prefer walking 6" off the ground, not as hard on my feet.

I must also tell you, regardless of the outcome, my love for you is not in vain. Just loving you, with hope in my heart the outcome is what I want is wonderful and I would not trade it for anything. Fox calls hope, faith's weak sister. I also have faith whatever the outcome, it will be in the highest good of all. Of course, if it's not what *I* want (and I think you want too) I won't understand it or like it. But that is the way it will be. I love you and must do the dishes. I'll probably write more during the game.

Love,

X

11/15/93 8:55 PM

Dearest Donna,

It's a funny thing. I try to pour out all my love for you on paper and there's always more left for you. Wow! This is neat stuff!

The smell of firewood and smoke and gardenias fill the air. The kind of neat moment I'd like to share with you. There will be more. With you, all my moments will be neat. Even the rough ones. You are in my heart. I want you in my arms.

Well, the Eagles are here and I'd better put the coffee on before I fall asleep. Of course, thinking about you keeps me awake. Maybe I can get into the game so I can go to sleep. Coffee time. Oh! Did I tell you about your gottawannas? You gottawanna bring me coffee in the morning. You don't necessarily have to do it, you just gottawanna. Now, what is your gottawanna for me?

Coffee's on. Dishes dried and away. PHI - 0, MIA - 7.
And now you are up to date. The hole where my tooth was, feels
great. Did I tell you recently I love you? Yes, I did. Darn. If
you mind me repeating myself, you'll have to tell me.

I do like the image of you dressed in your hair. (I'll blow
dry it for you, if you like.) Fresh from our shower. Washing all
the old away, beginning new as one. Honey, I think I will be so
awe struck, I won't know what to do. I'll just stand there and
drink you in, wondering how God could be so good to me. Even
now, you are a blessing in my life.

It is as I knew it would be. Your love, even from where
you are, makes me more than I am because I have more than I
have alone. I pray my love for you makes you more . . . more
what I don't know. But whatever, it is given freely to nourish
you. Just think . . . no, feel. Can you feel the power? I'm tearing
at you again. I regret I'm not sorry for it. Perhaps you have not
considered yourself as having value. You are extremely valuable
to me. You are precious. I cherish what I have with you. I want
more of you to love and cherish. I want to hold you while you
giggle, while you cry, while you just lay still smiling in the
contentment of being with me as I am with you. I want to
experience everything with you, for with you it will be all new.
I love you,
X

11/16/93 6 AM

Dearest Donna,
Darn blankets! It was really good snuggling weather last
night. We did not do as well with the Eagles last night as the
Steelers did with the Bills last Sunday. But, 19 - 14 is a win. I
like waking up loving you. Wish you were here.

It's weird. All my logic, intellectual power (Ho Ho) and
love cannot move you. Nor can yours. A sign will be provided.
Then you will be here. It will come at exactly the right time. It
always does. By the way, another of your abilities I love is the
ability to see and act on these signs. Or not act, as the case may
be - darn it!

The first time I saw you, I was coming from Domino's, and you were walking from the donut shop back to the paint store. I said to myself, "Wow! She's perfect." Then I went into the store and saw your rings. I was disappointed. Then I said, "Dummy. Any woman as beautiful as she is, is bound to be taken." Over the years I have known you, I discovered the source of your beauty is from within. It is the kind improving with age. You, my Dearest, are rare among women. Your love for me is a manifestation of God's love for me. I am blessed, and I know it. I think I am beginning to understand "grace." I have done little to deserve either God's love or yours, yet they are both present in my life. Until you came along, I didn't think anything in life could be more wonderful than my children. Wrong again. I love you.
X

9:30
Dearest Donna,

I saw you today. You are so amazing! I know of the struggle you are in. It is me on the wrong side of the counter multiplied by one thousand. (It is the wrong side because you are not there.) We have the same struggle, only yours is much more intense.

An hour or so - no, it was a half hour; I'm getting better - after I left you it dawned on me, I could be the sign you are looking for. I came home and wrote down the parable of Farmer Brown. There is me (rowboat), the love you are holding back (the speed boat) and what you hold deep in your soul (the chopper.) I only ask you be open to the idea. Is the message the messenger? Is the messenger the message?

I don't know how or why you became so valuable to me. It simply started because I thought you had the most perfect body I had ever seen. Then, your face was so beautiful too. I kind of knew, but it took me a while to figure out it was radiance from within giving you your beauty. I see it! You are so easy for me to respect and admire. Then, I felt your love - I thought it was desire or desire plus, until Roberta pointed it out. Yet it gave me something I never had before. At least I wasn't ready to feel it before you came into my life. It's hard to believe your High

School counselor told you at age 15, you were one of the coldest, hardest girls he had ever met. All the love I have seen pouring out of you towards everybody tells me you really turned around. Neat, isn't it?

I don't even know what the hell I'm doing here?   But here I am, miserably happy, Happily miserable. It is a wonderful new experience. Roberta told me we just have no control over who it is with whom we fall in love. I'm glad (for the most part) we can control our behavior, if not our hearts.

Do you remember the poem I wrote about us as David and Bathsheba? Where David screwed-up is his desire overrode his love and Bathsheba simply yielded to the King. Now, Kings are desirable, power as an aphrodisiac and all, but Bathsheba's husband, Uriah, was a General. No slouch at power himself! So Bathsheba wasn't really desirous of David.   He was the King. She yielded to his command.

His life sucked thereafter. Absolom, his son, tried to kill him. His son by Bathsheba died, and on and on and on. Honey, my love for you comforts me while my desire drives me nuts! Anyway, I read the book and don't want that ending in my life. There are differences. You have desire as do I. Both of us know what happens if we let the desire override our love. Oops! David double dipped his screw-up by having Uriah killed. I have friends in low places, but it is not necessary. The White Lady will win. You and I need do nothing except what we are doing. God will handle it in His time in a way in keeping with His plans for us. I surely hope mine are in sync with His. If not, it won't be the first time.

Precious one, I love you deeply. No matter what happens, that won't change. You are one in three billion. There is no other like you. Should God's plans and mine be different, it will be impossible for us to continue as "friends." At least for an undetermined period of time. If this is pressure, so be it. It is also reality and neither of us can have it both ways. Please don't consider it as an option. I won't be able to handle it. Grieving this loss, with you still there is too much to handle. It will be tough with you out of sight. Donna, you know better! Just as everything else I've ever said, you knew. I wonder if loving you is so easy because it's like loving me??? I have never come across a better fit in my life. No wonder God laughs so hard at us. Hey! I just thought of another reason. We could keep God in belly laughs for the rest of our lives and join in too!

Well, my Dearest one, I shall try and set my desire aside and be comforted in my love for you, and yours for me. That's nice.
Love,
X

THE PARABLE OF FARMER BROWN

Farmer Brown was plowing the field one day when he suffered a heart attack. He died, of course. When he reached the Pearly Gates, St. Peter asked, "What are you doing here. It is not your time yet. Return, and God will take care of you."

Farmer Brown returned, rested for a while, went back to work and prospered in his fields. Years later, the dam broke and the entire valley began to flood. The water was up to Farmer Brown's porch. A neighbor came by in a rowboat and cried out, "Farmer Brown, get in the boat and I will carry you to safety."

Farmer Brown refused saying, "No thank you, God will take care of me."

The water climbed higher forcing Farmer Brown to his porch roof. The sheriff came by in a big speed boat and yelled, "Farmer Brown, get in the boat and we will carry you to safety."

Farmer Brown again replied, "No thank you, God will take care of me."

Finally Farmer Brown climbed to the top of the roof and was holding on to the weather vane as the rushing water tried to sweep him away. A National Guard helicopter fluttered overhead, and a voice through a megaphone said, Farmer Brown, grab the ladder we have lowered and we will pull you to safety."

For the third time, Farmer Brown refused saying, "No thank you, God will take care of me."

Once again, Farmer Brown found himself at the Pearly Gates. This time in dismay he cried to St. Peter, "I thought you said you were going to take care of me."

St. Peter haughtily replied, "We sent you two boats and a chopper. What did you expect?"

Anon.

5:20 PM
Dearest Donna,

I am still angry with myself. I saw you today - gave you the parable - told you again I loved you and we could not be friends because of what is between us. I would be your enemy. Every time we looked at each other or talked with each other it would trigger the memories of our desire. This would destroy what you would be working toward. Wouldn't help me much either.

Feeling anger helps. I'm angry because you did not share with me your loss of child support. Share with me, damn it! That is what this is all about. I know how dependant you are on this money. Christmas time. Fear. Share it with me. I am here to share life with you. The good, the bad, the joyous, everything. Damn it, if you can't share with me, can you be a partner? ! You may lock me away, but don't lock me out. That will be your loss.

6:50   I'm going to Samantha's dress rehearsal for her play. We could have gone. We could have done a lot of things. Donna, you know what you have. You have a pretty good idea of what you'll be getting when you move. It was August 14, then September 14, then the Minister, now, wait through the Holidays? If I am to wait, then you are to communicate. I wait. You talk. No problem. Our value together lies in our ability to communicate. You want to take it away from me? And you? It is the biggest gift we bring to our table.

Dearest one, I'm glad we can both look in the mirror. Neither one of us has done anything to be ashamed of.
I love you.
X

11:30 I'm here. My false anger keeps me from feeling the pain of possibly losing you. Don't worry Right now you hold the key and when you look at me and say, "I love you," I just feel all loosey goosey going fluid like honey in a bon fire. I had a skinny HB at the Steak and Shake and am still hungry, but it is nothing compared to my hunger for you. I know you love me, I just need to hear you say it. And in case you hadn't guessed it by now, I

love you. Good night my sweet love. If it helps you to sleep,
know I love you and may that love comfort you.
X

11/18/93 6 PM

Dearest Donna,
		No message. No sign you were here to read the letters in
the sock drawer. How are you?   How are you coping with the
lost child support? Talk to me. Honey, I know you are hurting.
I cannot help it if you do not talk with me. This is one of the
most important things we have going. You talk. I listen. I really
listen to you. You are in your way very smart and I enjoy
pointing it out to you. I love watching you act on it and I am so
proud of you as just a wonderful human being. (Of course, it
doesn't hurt I would love to ravage your body.)
		Our communication is so empowering. Please don't take
it away. Can you talk with me without "slipping?" Without
further cracking the dammed up love behind your wall? OK, so
you can't. What is happening to you in your self-imposed
prison? I can see you being torn into little pieces from the inside.
Part of me wants to snatch you up by the hair and drag you off
caveman style; make your decision for you. Primal urges are
nice, I guess, but I hold you in too high a regard. You must make
your own decision, coming to it from within.
		Another part of me wants me to forget about you, not
talk or write, maybe go to Denver for a while. Because I love
you and hate to see you torn this way. (Don't worry, I don't think
I could afford to go to Vero, much less Denver.) So, I don't
know what to do. You tell me to stay away until after the
Holidays. Aug. Sept. Oct. Nov. Jan.? This is not a good pattern
for us to begin with. Is it?
		Honey, I don't have much time to give. I am of an age
where it is use it or lose it. I haven't used it in a while and really
have no desire to use it anywhere, except with you. I have my
fears too. I need exercise in that area, and you and your love
takes 20 or 30 years off. You hold the key. If you drop it . . . I
am afraid. But, this is my fear. I think I once told you the largest

and most sensitive erogenous zone is between the ears. So what
went on there before you, is not your responsibility You can take
full responsibility for the good stuff going on there now.

Ah well. I certainly hope this is the 2d "down period"
Ray predicted.

I will call you tomorrow, as your friend, because I love
you. If I know you as well as I think I do, you will have
probably already figured out a way of dealing with this shortfall.
With all else going on, maybe not. I think you are pretty human
and when a lot of excrement hits the whirling blades all at once,
most of us can get pretty overwhelmed. So, I'll call and see if we
can set aside our stuff for a moment, and just deal with your stuff
here. It won't be "we" as much as it will be you. I know you
have the strength and smarts to handle it, I just want to remind
you of it. As your friend, because I love you.
X

REGARDLESS

The long Fall doth chilly Winter bring
Followed true by dim and solemn Spring.
For light shineth not without my love
Regardless how high the sun above.

I wait her voice's tinkling sound
Like Heaven's bells around, around.
Yet silence is my companion fair
I'll ne'er forget her sweet shining hair.

Thunderous silence; Hell's gates roar.
Oh pray, Oh pray, this silence more
Shall end, and dulcet laughter take its place;
Once again, her beauteous face.

Her eyes so soft with love's damp tear
Yet strong enough to confound her fear.
And skin as smooth as baby's arm,
She woos me with her silent charm.

My rapture gone! Fall doth Winter bring
Followed true by dim and solemn Spring.
For light shineth not without my love
Regardless how high the sun above.

11/18/93

11/19/93 3:15 PM

Dearest, Dearest Donna,

You asked him if on a cruise far at sea, you and a kilo of cocaine fell overboard, which would he save? And he thought about it! You have given me my answer and my life. Now, it is but a matter of time. It is so funny we both had the same question to ask him. God! I love you. Your strength is phenomenal! We think so much alike it is almost scary, except I find it delightfully funny.

God loves me a lot. First my children, now you. What blessings I have! I am so proud of you. Your extra effort with him is so reassuring to me. No matter what happens, you will succeed. You have already gone beyond the extra mile, and a very small part of me wished for it to work. I like seeing miracles. The other miracle is you in my life. (That's the big part of me.)

Honey, I have plans. I plan to enjoy life with you. How, where, when with what, I have absolutely no idea. and don't really care. I think the two of us together will know or be given ways and means. You are the ground for my zillion volt battery. Thank you. (That one is for God.) Thank you. (That one is for you.)

I feel like a kid in a candy store, or maybe outside watching the shopkeeper stir about before he opens the door. I'm excited! Anticipating! Waiting for you with open arms.
I love you.
X

11/20/93 Midnight

Dearest Donna,

I did today what I hoped for you. I rested. I read my latest issue of *Poetry Pilot* dozed, wrote a poem. Basically I did nothing - I did write a letter to them complaining about poetic inbreeding. I left my Suzie housewife work undone - I'll get it tomorrow. I cooked up some frozen chicken soup for Sam, she opens tonight, and had to wash her darn dishes again!

But of all the things I did or did not do, talking with you brought overwhelming joy into my life. If I cry when I see you next, you'll know why. Honey, you are such a magnificent woman! I love just about everything about you. No, let's say everything about you I know I love. I love it so much if there is anything about you I don't know, will it make any difference? I doubt it.

I wonder if I have the words to express my admiration, respect and love for you. I can probably do a pretty good job with desire. It's the other stuff that is so wonderful, and you make it that way. Loving me the way you do. I also see here you clearing the decks. No baggage, guilt or any feelings getting in the way of us. I never thought of that, till now! . This, of course, puts you higher in my esteem. Wow! It now becomes obvious you know more about this stuff than do I, and I now become anxious to learn from you. You will find a willing pupil. How did I get so smart to pick you? ? Damn, I'm brilliant! Whatever I did to deserve you must have been fantastic. I must have saved planet Earth in another lifetime, Keeping God supplied with laughter at we mortals, and you are my reward. Nothing less would suffice. I love you the best and most I can. Teach me more.
  X

WORD FAILURE

Words, the poet's brush
painting pictures of life
using texture, color
impression, perception
from inside out or outside in.

Words fail
when life brings moments
wonderfully huge
beautifully terrifying
so immense no words
can convey confused joy
grieving in reverse
gain so magnificent
all the world's words
seem lacking.
Yet, perhaps
it is poet's lack, or shock,
or trauma or simply . . .
Overwhelming love.

11/19/93

11/20/93 7 AM

Dearest Donna,

Honey, I feel so dumb. I love you so much and feel almost unworthy of what you are doing for yourself and us. You are so darn smart, working the way you are, cutting these strings to the past, coming to me free. I am in awe of your love for me. I finally understand. I told you it would take a 2 x 4. So when are you going to teach me? I feel like a three year old, rapidly jumping up and down with joy. Ooooh! What comes next? Ooooh! This is so much fun.

I guess the only way I can show you my love at this time is to keep writing to you. Letting you know what is going on inside me and what is going on outside. This is something you can't do with me right now, and finally I'm catching on.

I hope these outpourings are adequate. I am so stunned with this new discovery. If anyone had ever loved me like this before, I was not aware of it. I don't think so. This is so wonderful. I want to let you know how much I appreciate it, and cherish it. It's such an enormous gift. I'm crying!

It is as though you fill every nook and cranny of my essence, and it never happened before. It is overwhelming. So the tears on my face are of gratitude and joy, and precious one, I feel so much more yet to come. I am glad I'm beginning to get used to it. Whatever you have for me I will accept, but as you can see, it may take me a while to catch on.

I love you.

X

8:45 PM

Dearest Donna,

I just returned from EnviroFest and found I was published in their magazine. Couples strolled, arm in arm, hand in hand, and I missed you so much. Were Sam not on, I could have gone with her; Tiffany is or will be there with her sister. Tiffany's boyfriend arrives Wednesday. Sam's doesn't get here 'till May and I have no idea when you'll be free.

I'm so tired. Being overwhelmed is draining. I planned to stay for the show, but was too tired. My ground wire came loose again.

It is strange. I sit here wondering if I am worthy of you. I never have been loved like this before. Am I walking the walk I talk? I know God thinks so or He wouldn't have put me in your life or you in mine. So I have to trust Him. I want to be with you so badly, I don't trust me.

Roger and his wife - a couple from Church and Roger was my student when I taught college years ago - were there. She is - like you - very beautiful. I guess that is when I missed you so much. I mean, it's always there, just sometimes more.

Honey, right now, this is all I can give you. I don't know if it helps or hurts to put it all on paper. I just do because I love you.
X

11/20/93 11:20 PM

Dearest Donna,

Sometimes I think I write the same thing to you over and over, I love you. Go to the blackboard and write, "I love Donna" 500 times. I don't know. I see what you do. There are two Amazons and a troop of Valkyrie packed in your tiny frame. When the only thing I can do is wait, and wait, and wait, and wait. It seems so insignificant in comparison.

The bull paws the dusty earth in ring center. Dry air is charged, heavy with tension as La Matadora circles in the stands above. She is preparing, cleaning the seats, her dress, mantilla, and everything to be perfect for the snorting bull. He charges, lodging his horn in the arena wall, shaking the stands. He runs in circles, waiting La Matadora. Soon she will come. Come to dance with veil and castanets, heels clicking to a rhythm heard only by the two of them. The bull rises from his resting place, pawing the downbeat, red eyes fixed on the vision of loveliness, dancing love's dance toward him. Clumsily he moves all four legs in this new sacred rhythm, conquering her, as she conquered him.

Oh well, at least it's different.
I love you,
X

WHAT IS LOVE

what is love
that i am
so deserved and desired?
her months of ritual cleaning
no stone
or grain un-turned
protecting the shambles
of what never was.
freedom walks with her loss
in heart
mind
soul
no baggage!
i wept, sobbed
overwhelmed with significance
understanding arriving with tears.
better yet,
she does this for her
and us to be.
unknown ever
only dreamed
laughed at
like it really existed
prayed for
so it would.

now it is here.

help.

11/20/93

11/21/93 5:45 PM

Dearest Donna,
        When you lockout, you do it well. I asked for it. I
know. Be careful of what you ask for. Truth? I am deeply
appreciative of it. We discussed why. More truth? I hate it. I'm
beginning to get used to mixed emotions, but the stir fry is ready.

6:15 PM
        Burp! (Excuse me.) I'll do dishes later. It was so good
to talk with you. It was close to wonderful. It will be when you
unlock. I am glad you told me my love strengthens you and I
was doing a good job of loving you. I think so but it doesn't
make any difference if I don't know you know. Also, I am very
relieved to hear you say you are in love with me - I had to listen
closely to hear it in your voice, and your acknowledgment you
loved me deeply. It validated what I feel from you, behind your
wall.
        I know you are waiting on The Boss, and I have to wait
also. I dislike saying this, but you won't hear it now, I need you.
If I said it to you now, it would put undue pressure on you.
Sometimes, I want to. I want to take you in my arms so
badly . . . it's a bitch! I want to yell, "Take your damn rings off
and get in my shower!" There are other things difficult to
understand. Mixed messages. "I don't want to lead you on."
"Love will win out." "I'm not in love with him." "Your love
gives me strength." It's confusing. I've been confused before.
Not like this, but at least confusion is no stranger. Click!
        It just hit me. You have to tell me you "don't want to
lead me on" to protect your wall. Nanny nanny boo boo. Gotcha!
When The Boss tells you to make your decision, I have faith in
which direction you will go. This is one helluva ride!
        I will use Raymond's prediction and go with 12/7/93.
Pearl Harbor Day. That will be our day. You don't know this
yet. I might let it slip. If I do, it might ruin the chance of it
coming sooner.
        Did I hear you right? It's hard to tell over the phone.
You are trying to force him to decide? If that is what I heard, we
may have a problem here. You can leave. You have good will.

What he has is his problem. You can't make him decide anything. Is this so you don't feel guilty? About what? He deceived you, remember? We need to talk about this.

8:20   I'm sort of cleaning up the kitchen, watching TV, wishin' you were here just snugglin' up next to me. We can snuggle almost as much as we can have fun in bed. I like snugglin'! I especially like snugglin' with someone that fits, and I've never met a better fit than you. I've known you were perfect for me since I laid eyes on you. You are a perfect fit. And you were worried about how tall I was. I'm still tall, You are no longer worried. It works. Donna, love, you know a lot of things. I respect that. Let me know some things too. I don't mean all the stuff I've read, but the stuff in my gut. I have rare but solid contact. When I have the glancing blows, I need your validation so the contact will improve. One of the things I know is you can do this.

Ya see, it's more than a snugglin' fit we have. Snugglin' is just an outside way of showin' how well we fit inside. I know you figured that out. I know how smart you are.

Honey, writing to you, I guess letting you know I'm thinking about you, even though you won't really know until you read this. You know now, this will validate what you already know. Something tangible. I love to validate you. It makes me feel smart. (Ho. Ho.) I'm glad you told me I was doing a good job of loving you. That's the easy part. At least what I'm feeling and doing is easy - except the waiting. Another reason for, or thing about, our fit.

Hey! If you are locked down, and still feel totally loved by me, how are you going to feel when you quit filtering it? Honey, what I feel about you, in you, from you, through me is wow-wonderful. When you unlock, it will be like the ring: unending, growing, strengthening circle of love. It's so neat. I keep putting it down on paper and the more I put the more there is. Because of you, I've tapped into the Infinite Love source. Thank you.

I don't want to say much more, I just want to snuggle with you. Hold you close. Touch you, to make sure you are real. You are really a new experience for me.

10:20   Well, I ate too much Chocolate Chip. The stove is clean
and the coffee"s on. I'd rather go to bed with you, but I'll stay up
and watch TV until I fall asleep. Sometimes I think this is all so
silly, but I know there is a reason. I don't know what it is
sometimes, like now when I'm tired. Most of the time I do. I
just love you so much. I hope it is for more than simply helping
you escape. But if that is all, it's OK. I don't like the idea, but so
what?
I love you.
X

WAITING AGAIN

As an impatient child
waits to go potty
eat desert
open a package
leave the corner
give a gift,
I wait for you.

As patient bear waits leaping salmon
hungry lion hides at water hole rushes
little bird is frozen by cat's eyes
I wait for you to feed me in ways
I knew not before, strengthening,
freeing my soul's wings that we may fly.

I pass time, rebuilding
fixing
cleaning
painting
and writing
inadequate metaphors
that nowhere nearly
reflect me.

11/21/93

11/22/93
Dearest Donna,

Here I go again. Now I'm mad. At me. One of the excuses I had to see you today was I had a poem published and I wanted to show you. I was bringing you a copy and forgot to give it to you. I take one look at you - I could see your sorrow - and everything else gets blown away. I felt like a house cat bringing a dead mouse to Mamma saying, "See what I did for you? Please scratch my ears. Purr." Oh well. I lost it. It was more important to hold you and hug you and stuff like that.

Sam gave me some cookies too. I was going to bring them in and offer you some. I was going to bring up my curried tuna fish salad and some crackers for you too. I forgot. All my gifts, I forgot. Being with you is just so important to me right now. (I'm eating the cookies. See how selfish I am?)

Well, it's 4:30 and I'm going to call you soon if you don't call me soon. Even on the telephone, I feel with you.

6 PM   Sam was here - needed a fry pan - I got the film in and I'll have it back tonight. Then I can look at you looking at me with all the love in your eyes. Wow! What will come out of my pen then?! Sam just called. More cookies. I'll leave some of those out for you too.

I'm so glad you told me about what was weighing heavy on your mind. My automatic response; "Unacceptable." As I told you, there are ways of dealing with these things. I know of some ways, but it doesn't mean squat. What counts is you don't want to do it any more. With that, we've got it made.

8 PM

Having our picture may be a screw up. I like looking at it. That's where you belong; right next to my heart. I was wrong about the eyes. You are of course hurting and transparent, yet I'm glad I'm there and I'm really glad I'm there.

I got two fortune cookies. I'll leave the fortunes out for you tomorrow. They're not very good. I know my hard work is paying off, and when you said we were going house shopping,

my luck changed. So, they're not very good. I knew that. I think
I will play their numbers on Lotto, though.

It was so wonderful being with you today. The few
minutes under Sam's chaperonage, and then on the phone. We
have such a fit. I don't really understand why we are so honest
with each other. I think it's trust. I trust you. I trust you to
follow your instincts, and I trust your instincts. On top of which,
you are pretty dad gum smart! (You have to be. You're picking
me.) No ego here, of course.

You will soon be free. Laugh. Share joy with me. We
won't settle for happiness. JOY.   Be alive with me. I love you.
Cry with me. I love you. Damn! We fit well together.
Love,
X

BE ALIVE

Be alive with me.
  Share the joy
of life anew,
sorrow
of losses fresh and past.
Do your toes
wiggle
as your eyes
twinkle?
  Laugh with me
at:
babies burping,
puppies playful,
sunsets serene and
waves walking
over the top of the ocean.
  A caress,
soft cheeks
that frame your smile.

Cry with me
at:
horrible hunger,
private pain,
torturous tragedy and
four fearful
horsemen.
* A full warm hug*
embraces
the child embodied in
the woman.
* Share God with me:*
infinite law, love, life,
truth, intelligence,
spirit, soul.
* A duet sung*
from the soul of love
to eternal goodness,
for as long as
consciousness is.
* Be alive with me.*

11/23/93

Dearest Donna,

Oh, Precious One! The flowers damn near brought me to tears. I've never been loved like this. You are wonderful. There is so much in my heart - it just keeps overflowing - I think for you, I know because of you. I was thinking we should have met 20 years ago. But, you wouldn't have gone for Plastic Man. I don't think I would have appreciated you for who and what you are then as I do now. So I'm very glad we met when we did. I was not ready to accept what you offer. I honestly wonder if I am now? I know I have the capacity, you will have to help me develop it.

Yes, my Dearest, I love you totally. All of you. The good, the bad and the ugly. (There is no ugly and damn little bad, but I will allow and accept your humanness as you have accepted mine.) You are so beautiful. I look at your picture and even with the pain in your eyes from your sister's words, you are beautiful. The pain is even beautiful because of its source, your good name. You care about yourself and that is beautiful. I love you from the tips of your unseen toes to the end of the longest strand of hair on your beautiful head. I love your heart and your soul. I admire your instincts and respect them. Yes, My Dearest, I love you totally.

I went over to Tiffany's to show her your picture. She has good vibes about us. She mostly talked about her boyfriend. Weird things are happening. Soul mates are finding each other. She wanted to show me some lingerie shoe bought to wear for him. I respectfully declined. I would have had to come club you over the head and drag you off to my cave. (I use Styrofoam clubs for this purpose.)

Damn woman! I wish you were here so we could talk. Then I wouldn't have to write all this. I could just tell you while I hold you, between hugs and kisses. I made the tea. I guess you noticed the jug was empty. Now I have to fold and hang the clothes. Be right back.

Oh, my precious Donna. I missed you. I thought of you as I folded clothes, as I ate my C.C. ice cream, as I washed the

tea pans, I thought of you. I think I'm in love with you! Tsk!
Tsk! I told Tiffany tonight, "I'm gone." I'm so far out on a limb;
I'm over an infinite abyss. Should the limb break, I would fall
forever. Your light, the light of your love guides me over the
abyss.

I put your flowers in a white bud vase. White is the sum
of all the colors, and I love you through each of them. I've told
you how smart you are. After all, you fell in love with me. But,
my precious child of God, I am brilliant! I fell in love with you.
It's past 11. The car is running. Not well; my mechanic jury
rigged it. Needs a muffler or something. I'll check it in the AM
Since you are not sleeping with me, sleep with my love wrapped
around you like a warm blanket bringing you peace and comfort.

I wanted to thank you for coming over today. I have so
much I want to share with you. Take whatever you need.
I love you.
X

11/24/93 7:45 AM

Dearest Donna,

I am still thrilled about your visit here yesterday in my
absence. The flowers thrive in their vase as I thrive on your love.
Part of me wishes you could have stayed longer, at least a
lifetime. - yet the rest of me knows why you could not.
Basically, mission accomplished. You know I love you and
reading the few pages you did, validated your internal
knowledge. I love to validate you! I guess you stopped before
getting overwhelmed. I had the tissues out in case.

I felt your presence when I came in at 7. It was a
wonderful feeling of love. Then I saw your note. I wondered
what in the hell you were talking about, "flowers?" Then I saw
them on my pillows. So beautiful. The thought. The touch.
God loves me an awful lot to put you in my life. You are exactly
what I asked for, and so much more. It's like buying a car and
finding out the gas, oil and everything are free for the rest of your
life. I know it's silly but when I asked God for a wonderful

woman, I guess I didn't know what wonderful really meant. Wow! You are so much more than I asked for. Hey! The Boss is really neat. Look what a bonus he gave me in you.

The car is at the muffler shop. It's right around the corner. I hope you looked in the Louise Hay book at what I highlighted. If not, I'll tell you when I call. Part of the emotional spiritual cycle of your illness is rejecting life. My experience tells me this happens when people feel like life, in the form of other people, has rejected them.

Donna, many who do not understand your special essence have rejected and shamed you. A rejection of life is simply a defense mechanism against the pain of being rejected by those you love. I understand a little about how special you are. I say "a little" because you keep surprising me. It will take a lifetime, and then I won't fully know. The bottom line here is I accept you, all of you, in a loving way I've never before had the pleasure of being acquainted with. So, put that in your pipe and smoke it!

The flip side of the coin is you do not have to accept the rejection. Remember who they are. Just sick people. As we reject others, we reject ourselves. They may never accept you. You can't make them. They do not have, or have not developed the capacity to really see who you are. So, my precious one, embrace life. All of it. Its pain and its sorrow. Its love and its joy. It is simply life. Part of which is simply a human experience for us to enjoy, to feel and to participate in. It's pretty short, so we have to take at what God gives us, and learn how to deal with it so we can enjoy it.
Love,
X

Dearest Donna,

I'm waiting for 4:30 to roll around so I can have my mechanic look at the car. It's like trying to pull a semi with an Escort! Anyway, you couldn't make it over and maybe that is for the best. I do have something to show you, but knowing us . . . Then you wouldn't be able to hold it together for tomorrow. I wish you could write to me and get this stuff out. I know mine keeps overflowing. It has spilled over 64 pages now. I hope you hear something soon. Hey, this helps me. I can't hold you or kiss you or even talk with you. Time, precious one, We need time together, because this time apart sucks!

It is so nice loving you, and being loved by you. Laughing when a stray "I love you" slips out from behind your dam of feelings. I know you are doing the right thing for you, and when it comes to pass, the right thing for us. I just wish it would come to pass more quickly.

I think soon I will start writing erotically. It seems your presence in my life has improved my testosterone level quite significantly. I'm beginning to respond as though I were half my age. Look out!!!

I trust you. I trust you to do what is right for you; not necessarily what you want to do. You have proved it to me. I believe when there is a more solid us, you will do what is right for us. I never met anybody I trust as much as you, and I have a few trusted friends. Honey, I also trust you to know whether we will be "right" together. Should your decision be no, you will not have betrayed my trust in you. I would be deeply saddened, of course, but that comes from expectations, not trust. I love you. Nap time then take the car in.

Boy, was I tired! Tiffany called at 4 and woke me up. She's on her way to pick up her boyfriend. I took the car in and the problem may be in a TPS connector. (Don't ask me.) Or the torque converter. The tranny is under warrantee Whew!

I think I'm supposed to cook since I missed Padrino's. I just want to be with you so badly, take you out of this stressful situation you are in and let you heal. I love you so much. I guess I'll cook.
Love,
X

10 PM
Dearest Donna,

This is a new kind of alone. Before, alone meant by myself, without someone, self enclosed, hoping what I believed, was in fact true. Now the word takes on a new significance, a deeper meaning, "a - lone." "A" means without. Sometimes, when in front of a vowel, "an" is used, like "anoxic, without life sustaining oxygen." Lone is one, singular, one. We are the one alone means now without the one we are creating. Alone. A void in life, a hole swallowing me like a tasty tidbit. Alone. Without myself.

It passes after its crescendo. Aloneness, as I regain a piece of me to hang onto once again. I heard today God created woman to help man, as equal partners. It is what I have been saying for a long time, and my partner came along and I thought she was another's. Then, hope: she wasn't really, then she loved me then . . . and I don't know, yet I do know and in knowing . . . it seems so silly sometimes and this is one of those times when I just don't know how much more I can take. I'm drowning in my pent up love for you. And you, is your dam ready to break, collapse?

I sit here reliving my fantasy made real by you, just snuggling in the chair, touching you, holding you, beaming as your eyes filled with love for me and you pressed in closer, seeking the warmth and comfort of my body; simply snuggling, touching, holding. I know I am loved. I know you love me. And yet it hurts - a new kind of agony being without you. Confusedly knowing you are where you are because you love me so deeply. And your pain? Your agony? I know it is there. I know you want me as badly, as wonderfully as I want you.

What it boils down to is I'm afraid of losing you. One way or another, I'm afraid. Then faith kicks in. Not in our love, which is beyond my comprehension, much less words, but in God. He always does what is best for us, whether we like it or not. God knows I don't like this! Yet, I love you so much, I must let you stay there, BECAUSE you love me. It's overwhelming! Maybe I can do something else for a while.
Love,
X

11/25/93 7:30 AM

Dearest Donna,

Yeah, I did something else for a while. Went to sleep. Wow. This stuff is draining. I didn't finish cleaning the kitchen (yuck!) or make my coffee. (Arrrgggg!) So anyway, Happy Turkey Day. I am very thankful you are in my life and my heart as I believe I am in yours. No, as I know I am in yours. I just don't know when and I want it now. (Wanhhh!)

So, here I am, dreaming about winning the Lotto to set us free. Our bankruptcies paid off, your support agreement modified to a trust account freeing you from #1, etc., etc. It's your freedom I want more than anything. Mine too. I guess it is a desire for greater purity in our love. We are both way beyond the purity of babes, yet our efforts in this relationship indicate our desire for righteousness and purity in all ways. So, maybe we can't have it. At least we can desire it.

Look ahead with me to a time where we can be together in peace and pleasantness, whether I win the Lotto or not. You are far more important in my life than a mere $15 million. With you I will be far richer than I already am with my children. I was wondering also, if I won, would this put more pressure on you, or would you see it as a sign to make your move? I know you are not for sale. I know you love me for who and what I am, certainly not how much money I have, or don't have as is the case. This is a part of your impressive uniqueness. It's me. Just as with me, it's you.

I mean, look at the outside of you. Four kids, two sour marriages, bankrupt. Damn! Why, you're just like me! Except, you were smarter. If I knew my kids were going to bring as much joy into my life as they have, I don't think I would have stopped at four, much less two. So, six is OK. (Heh. Heh. Heh. Six are great!)

Yet, my Precious One, I know what kind of partner you are and will be for me. We fit so well together. Hand in glove, nut and bolt holding the world together, a team, a working relationship, a perfect match coming only from a perfect source. I guess it has nothing to do with our "deserving" one another, as much as simply that is the way it is supposed to be. I can accept that. It's so much easier than creating stories about my saving mankind in an earlier lifetime and you are God's reward - but I won't let the thought go.

I love you and will send you more later. Believe it or not, I have other letters to write this morning - some cleaning and fixing to do, you know just stuff and I almost forgot the Ironing!
I love you,
X

2:30 PM

Well, Precious One, not to worry. I did not win the Lotto. One number out of 18. I'll play the same numbers again. We can use the extra $. If I don't check the numbers, then maybe I've won so I am a potential winner right up until I find out otherwise.

I had to put these letters in a folder. The envelope just wasn't cutting it anymore. It's just past half time and soon I'll have to get ready to go to Tiffany's. X Jr. was by and I showed him your picture. He said, "No wonder you are hanging around the paint store!" You are really beautiful.

I'm finally triggered out. I guess I'll get busy on some other things. The letters are written, the book is made. Time for more cleaning - I'll save the ironing for tonight.
I love you.
X
PS. I stuck the poetry and the note you wrote and just about everything into the book. Oops! I forgot your first note on the back of the check book deposit slip - yes, I kept that too. Oh well! I'm nuts. I love you. X
7 PM   I'm stuffed! I'm sorry precious one. I know inside and out you need your space to do what you need to do for you and for us. I'm trying my hardest and you make it so difficult. You and your damn dam! I want to scale the wall and dive into the pool of love behind it with the joy of a young boy rope swinging over a pond on a warm summer's day. I want to hold my breath and free dive to the bottom, stirring the mud with my feet and explode on through the surface like a great whale; splashing droplets of your love over the world, into the Cosmos from which it came. Fuck your wall! Your dam!

I pay homage at the foot, using every ounce of strength I have to hold me in place. Oh, God! Much easier scaling ropeless the vertical wall than staying here. And stay I must. The droplets splash over, wetting me, challenging me to stay or to climb. The ecstasy of being with you is sometimes beyond my comprehension. Your love - so much, so highly developed, yet so human and so desired. I may be the greatest lover you know, but you, Dearest are more loving than anyone I have ever known. I think we strike a chord resonating our harmonic frequency, our mutual harmonic frequency allowing and encouraging us to grow. Thank you for your strength or we could wind up like Galloping Gertie, the Tacoma Narrows bridge that collapsed in the 40's (I think) when the wind got it swinging in its natural harmonic frequency.

We reflect off each other like waves seiching in a bay, a natural phenomenon on the occurrence of the high tide as we seem to be at the high tide of love. And the wonderful thing about tide is just as soon as it goes out, it comes in again.
I love you.
X

10 PM
Dearest Donna,

The turkey finally did me in, and once again I crashed without finishing the kitchen stuff or making coffee. I've many habits needing change, however pre making my coffee is not one of them.

I'm glad I can describe the power of our love in terms of natural phenomenon. It feels so natural to me. As natural as a sunrise or clouds or stars. One of the things bothering me so much is your unwillingness to share with me what you are going through at this time. I know you can. I think you want to. And I know if you do, it will break or at least weaken your wall. On those rare and special times I see you for a minute or two, you tell me of some new pain you and The Boss are handling. I feel left out. I am left out. Soon I hope you will realize your powerlessness in your situation and get out; not for me, but for yourself.

Honey, when I read my work to an audience, many clap
politely. But at least one hears my words and takes them in,
either with laughter or sorrow. I write and read with depth from
different places; my heart my soul, or even my head, and
occasionally my loins. Sometimes, I reach a lot of people.
Sometimes only one. There are always those who are in a
different place than I am when I read, and they don't hear. They
are supposed to be where they are.   It's no big deal. As the Book
says, you shake the dust off your feet and keep on traveling.
        Your "legal partner" doesn't get the message. Neither
did Pharaoh, and he had ten plagues! When he finally let them
go, he changed his mind and chased them down. Oops! He
never really got the message. Neither does Ralph.
I love you.
X

11/26/93 6 PM

Dearest Donna,
        I'm pissed. Which is another way of saying hurt. Today
on the phone after telling me you were overwhelmed, you said
for the first time, "go or stay." You never said "stay" before.
        First, I'm not taking responsibility for your being
overwhelmed. It's your feeling, probably from fighting what you
know with some screwed up sense of duty. I'm going to throw
your words back at you. You "love and want me more than
you've ever wanted anybody." You are, "deeply in love with
me." I know this. I've never been loved the way you love me.
Nor have I ever loved anybody the way I love you.
        I feel like you are ready to throw God's gift to us away.
This isn't about me or you, it is about what is between us. That
which makes our massive chemistry pale to insignificance; that
which gives our chemistry its significance. That which is God's
gift to us. He bestows it between us, not on one or the other.
        You never again will have what we have, nor will I. It is
a deep loss, unfathomable. I feel it is gone. I won't bother you
any more. (Of course I'm lying.) No, it is not gone I think

you've already made up your mind. To hide it away further. I'm
sorry for both of us. I will not condone or enable your medicinal
pot use. I will provide an environment where it is not necessary.
If that is not good enough, I'm again sorry for both of us. It's
obviously your choice. I think you've made it.
Ciao,
X

11/27/93 2 PM

Dearest Donna,
        I believe you have decided to stay. I cried my self to
sleep last night and slept for an unaccustomed 8 hours. Today I
made my peace with the Boss. There is no doubt in my mind our
love was His gift. I am not a "great lover," I was simply
honoring His gift to us. I did the best I could, The Boss knows
who and what I am, as he knows who and what you are, and all
of us are. You see God in me? It's not me; it is us.
        The Gift is precious to me. Never having been loved
before the way you love me, I cannot comprehend its having a
human source; it was sacred. Still is. Probably always will be. I
grieve the loss of my expectation sorely. I must now with draw
for my own protection. I don't know what for. Protection of
what? Guardian of a love that will never be? Consummated?
The love is there. That stays. Once the Boss puts something in
motion, it's like the bunny that keeps going and going and going.
        My expectation now is by the time we next talk - I think
you'll call - you will have gone back to Ralph, consummating the
fraud. It is not fraud anymore, because now you know. So, our
window of opportunity is gone and you are once again a married
woman and off limits. Does this stop me from loving you? No,
only it can only be felt rather than displayed.
        If my expectation is correct, you will have made a
choice. I will honor your choice, as I honored His gift. I believe
this was a once in a lifetime gift. We get one opportunity for the
brass (in this case, gold) ring for one turn of the Carrousel. I
have a lot of faith is God, but He out did himself when he put
you in my life. It would be sacrilegious for me to ask again.
(Hey God, can you top this?)

Maybe, just maybe, I can find the skill to share a glimpse
of what we have with others to let them know it is real, it does
exist and it is more beautiful and wondrous than they can
imagine or I can describe. And for God's sake, do not let it go. It
is what life is all about, this accepting of God's gifts to us. And
once this happens, His gifts keep on coming!

They say,"write about what you know." Now, I know.
Should only one glean partial insight of what we have, his or her
life will be enhanced. I could write about the depths of my grief
for the bottom dwellers, but why, when I may be able to share
this joy? The Prophet says something about the cup holding joy
is hollowed by sorrow. Then my joy is infinite . . .
I love you always,
X

11/28/93 11 PM

Dearest Donna,

I wasn't going to write you any more. Like, I wasn't
going to love you anymore. I am so confused. I feel like I'm
being used. Not by you. By God. The power of this love I have
for you is beyond my comprehension as is what I feel from you.
I want to go with it. You can't. Is it tougher on you than on me?
I don't think so. It's tough on both of us, and neither of us has it
one iota easier than the other.

No, maybe I do have it easier. I have the luxury of
expressing my feelings on paper. When you call, I can openly
and honestly attempt to tell you how much I love you. You can't.
You have to swallow it. Choke it back to keep your focus. I
would burst into spontaneous flame were I to attempt to do what
you are doing. So yes, you have it more difficult than I. And I
am nuts!

Anyway, if I am correct and the fates smile, we will be
together soon - whatever that is. If I am not, we won't. I will
have missed the brass (gold) ring this time around and will have
to wait to grab it the next time. Maybe you'll be there too. Of
course you will. This life. Next life. Maybe both.

Honey, I'm obviously not capable of loving you the way
I do, and I have to wonder if mere mortal woman is capable of
loving me the way you do. So consider we are both simply
instruments to reward each other. I have to cop out. I'm crazy
enough as it is.
Love,
X

MORE WAITING

Smoking sitting watching TV
Wondering when she'll come to me

Halloween, Turkey Day come, go
Time is certainly passing slow.

Change, divorce grieving healing
What cards are these life is dealing?

This power, love patience required
My feet in muck feel like they're mired.

I'm waiting for my love and yet...
Oh Hell! I'll have a cigarette.

11/29/93

Dearest Donna,
        I'm trying to figure out how to wrap this up. You are
now another beautiful married woman. A woman to be admired
from a respectful distance. Unfortunately, it will have to be a
long distance. There is no profit in our torturing each other.
        Oh, by the way, will you please return my heart? I gave
it to you and I know you treated it with loving kindness. I'm sure

68

it will be better for having been in your care. I hope yours is better also for having been in mine.

This has been the most wonderful experience in my life and I thank you for it. It was a gift I shall always honor and cherish. You brought a new and deeper meaning of the word love into my life. I felt the depth of the roots and looked forward to its - to our growing with it. Maybe it is best this one great love came late for me. Had it come early, it would only mean more time spent grieving its loss. Yuck!

The word love for me always had something missing. Many times it felt shallow escaping my lips, like I found it floating in the back of my mouth and spat it out. Or when I wrote of it, it was like three quarters of a pie. Oh, a big pie, yet with some of it missing. Thanks to you, I have the whole pie now. I wish there was something I could do with it.

I'm glad you feel things are working out for you. I wish you the best with your choice. I will always love you, if nothing more, simply for the wonderful woman you are. Although at this time I have absolutely no idea where else I would be, I will not promise to be "there" for you. I cannot believe anyone could ever take your place in my heart. You have treated it with too much kindness, love and respect. Yet if I tell you I will always be there for you, it could put a wedge in what you need to do. Now, if things change for you, please find some way of letting me know. Who knows where I'll be? My phone might even still work. God speed you on your journey.
Love,
X

12/1/93

Dearest Donna,

I'm watching Lethal Weapon (again) where Mel is putting a gun in his mouth over the loss of his wife. I identify with the feelings. The sorrow! God! It hurts! I know I'd feel better if you were just out of the clusterfuck you are in! I'd feel even better if you were here. But you are not.

I may not see you. I may not be with you - in person -
but I love you. I almost wish I didn't and you didn't. I know this
hurts you too. I have never minded pain. It's nearly - not quite -
unbearable. It's suffering that ticks me off! You are and I am.

I can go on, focusing on the pain I feel, but why? I
would rather focus on the wonderful thing between us: God's gift.
Honey like I said, part of me wishes it would go away. No I
know God knows what he is doing, even if we don't. I'm sure
He's laughing at us, our lack of faith - at least mine. I regret to
advise you I see no other end than our being together. There is a
problem though. I don't see when.

I think we could make love for a year or two without
getting tired. We can laugh together with the joy of our oneness.
It is so bottled up in me and just keeps running off on paper. I
quit.
Love,
X

12/2/93 6:30 PM

Dearest Donna,
Your turn for flowers today. Same as you left on my
pillow. I've been wanting to do this for months. I said "to hell
with it " and did it. I knew you'd know. No card was necessary.
Your phone message is saved. I play it again and again just to
hear you say, "I love you."

I quit trying to turn myself off from you. Whatever I do
doesn't seem to work. Maybe I should join another 12-step
program? Nah. Were I addicted to you, I'd be parked across the
street with field glasses, I'd find out where you live and all sort
of stuff. I think I respect me and my rights and you and your
rights too much. It is simply love. Damn!

I'm glad the flowers made your day. I love making your
day and I'd like to make the rest of them too. But . . .

Honey, what you told me today does scare me. First,
when you said if you see him just after talking to me, you feel
like you are cheating on him. Well, then you are. Emotional
fidelity is as important as physical fidelity in a marriage. You

don't have it because you are in love with me. Frankly, I was hoping it was the other way around; you felt like you were cheating on me. You have made a decision; you are still married. Another Damn!

Next - and I asked you not to answer this because either way it would hurt - you said his love making was different, better, not crack oriented. Let me thank you for honestly validating what I knew about Thanksgiving. A very small part of me is happy for you. You deserve the very best. At least you're getting better than you had. Most of me weeps you went back . . . knowing.

The other side of the coin is you are now aware of the difference. I was hoping it would be I who showed you.

Of course, then, there was the fantasy you let yourself have about running up my driveway into my arms and knocking me over. Thank you for thinking of me - no, for allowing your self *those* thoughts about me. I know you've been thinking about me in spite of your self. I know how hard it is to try and not think about, fantasize about you. I guess that is why I write these letters. This way, we are more real for me. No . . . wrong. We **are** real. You are not physically here yet.

I'm sorry you were cornered into the situation, yet there are a lot of positive things there. Your desire for family I think beautiful. Me too, only I had to choose one over many years. My kids are wonderful. That's easy. Sam is a sister, Roberta a younger wise aunt. And many other friends who over the years have gained my trust and respect to become almost a family. I would love to share them with you as I have Roberta and Sam. Honey, your in-law family is very sick and you deserve much better. Yet if they can affect you . . . ? Are you that hungry for acceptance? I offer it freely. It comes with loving you.

Honey, I understand your commitment to marriage. Are you cheating on him, or your commitment to marriage? I took a C.C. break and ate too much and I've got the chills. It's 9 PM and I'm exhausted. This is so draining. But, I love you.
X

12/3/93 6 AM

Dearest Donna,

I've been awake for a couple of hours - thinking about you, about us. I feel a little betrayed because you closed our window of opportunity. It is stupid because you are married to him. It is worse because you are in love with me. You have to fight that love and shut it out to be with him.

Yesterday, when I told you I loved you more than anything in this world, you said, "that's the way it's supposed to be." No, were you here, with me and loved me as you do, **that** is the way it is supposed to be. This is wrong for both of us. You are honoring a commitment to betrayal. Where is it right for me to do this? Perhaps our strength lies in our weaknesses? We are simply human after all.

Joseph in the pit, Daniel in the lion's den, Joshua in the belly of a whale, and you in a clusterfuck! There is precedent. Your words on my answering machine, "I'm coming to you, soon, I love you," sweetly echo in my head as a part of the mass confusion reigning there. Part of me feels like I'm being drawn into your situation, and that won't happen! I've worked too hard to find out who I am, to be open, to feel, to love. Were I there, I could not enjoy loving you as I do, and I enjoy loving you.

I have to pick up my son and go to work - more later.
I love you.
X

8 AM
Quickie. Damn, I raised a smart kid! I told him this was driving me nuts. He says, "Hold back and stay available. Of course that's easier said from my seat than yours." I told him that's what everybody says. He says, "Everybody's right." Oh well. See you later, on paper anyway.
X

5:20 PM

Hi Honey,

We spoke on the phone and I said last call? And you said yes and got off the phone too quickly as he walked in. Then you called back while I was outside trimming and erased your earlier message from Tuesday. I saved it and listened to it over and over; "thank you. I love you. The Boss loves you. Keep smiling." I played it again when I came in and forgot to save it. Then you called to say good bye, and I saved it. At least it is the sound of your voice. Oh, I'll forget to save it again and it will get erased.

Well, now we are going to see how much I love you. Probably not too much. As a child I learned "love is staying away." As an adult, I finally learned differently. Now I must revert until you say the White Lady won. How long will it take? How much can I take? I have to assume we are over. Unnhhh. A fist in the gut! Well honey, you do what you have to do and we'll see how many more times you cut the rope before he hangs himself.

No! You cannot have a combination of us. He is him and I am me. I have my drawbacks too, and I have my good points, and so do you. Because of you, I have accepted many things I know before you, I would not tolerate. You seem to make them pale into insignificance. Like I said, some force other than anything I have ever known before is driving me. So put all this behind you and call.

Love,

X.

STRANGE WAYS

An opportunity seized
A moment who then seized me.
As in an angry dog's jaws
shredded like a rag doll free.

A simple kiss or two I stole
From a beauty who asked me to
In unspoken words she asked it
I did it; first one and then two.

It was at first as friends we were
But it grew and it grew and grew.
'Till we found ourselves embracing;
Please God, I never, never knew.

Knowing she had a husband, of sorts
I stayed back as far as I could.
Then she said she was leaving him
I rejoiced as I knew I would.

Never been loved like this before
So much, so good; I feel the dance.
I've never loved like this before...
Then she gave him a second chance.

Rationalizing is what I do
And I do it very well.
Thank God I'm so good at it
Dangling over the abyss of Hell.

Maybe she wants him to hang himself
She's giving plenty of rope.
I've had my last call to her
And with it most of my hope.

I broke a cardinal rule you see
Married women are taboo
Falling in love brings naught but pain
Intense pain for me and you.

I wonder if the game is over?
Did the fat lady really sing?
Or is she doing this to see
If she can accept my ring?

From everything to nothing
It happened overnight.
Nietzsche laughs abundantly
With my visage in his sight.

"I told you of the illusion
You fell for it anyway.
Damned romantic poet,
In Hell your life will stay!

"Perhaps, yet look where I have been
The gates of Heaven far behind.
I've had knowledge you'll never know
and joy beyond your mind.

"For if pain's the price of having joy
I'll take it any day.
Passionate extremes are life's great gift.
And you sir, won't stand in my way."

Right now I feel very flat
As a parched desert plain.
The gift betrayed as it had to be:
Life is very strange.

12/6/93 8:45 PM

My Dearest, Dearest Donna,
        I can't stand it! Not writing to you. What a wonderful
day! I went in to tell you we should not see each other or talk
again until you took your wedding rings off, so you took them
off. I had no idea what had happened, but I'm so joyous you are
finally free. I say this knowing the freedom is in your heart and
it will take a while for it to sink in between your ears. Then the
healing and the paper work and court and all the stuff.
        My precious one, My Gift, your freedom is the real gift.
I know what a wonderful woman you are. But right now, I'm out
of C.C. Be back in a minute.
        Much better! I found a couple of chocolate nuggets in
with the chips. Kinda like you. A golden nugget among the
fool's-gold flakes. Except, your love is more precious than gold.
        I told you today you are responsible for your behavior,
not my feelings. However, your behavior today brought great
joy into my life. You were so funny, with your arms jerking out
a couple of inches, then back, controlling a nearly uncontrollable
urge to hug me. When you finally did, it was beautiful and I felt
the power.
        Well, My Dearest, I have waited for you a long time.
You are finally on the path to freedom, where you will be free to
choose. Till then, we can be the best of friends, while I love you
more than anything on this earth. I love you.
X
PS. Sam and I saw the psychic on November 6, not November 7
as I thought before. Strange.
X

12/8/93 11 AM

Dearest Donna,
        The waiting is over. You are not here with me, but you
have taken the first step. Now the period of insanity begins, with
your emotions and worries going nutso. And here is where I

retreat back to being your friend, with ulterior motives. I'll be
here to help you laugh at your own insanity, maybe throw in
some of mine for an extra laugh.

I'll make suggestions - as I did this morning on the
phone - most of which you will have already thought of, but it
will validate your thinking. Damn! you are stronger than I
realized.

Waiting now is a lot easier since the process began. And
it's easier to be your friend (with motives). I see you on the path
to your freedom and that is good. I'm relaxed about this now. A
little worried, yes, about you. But much more relaxed.
Of course it could change in a few days, or hours, or minutes, but
right now, everything is cool on this end. Nothing's gone away: I
have confidence in your ability to handle things. You are one
hell of a woman!
Love,
X

12/9/93 6 PM
Hi Honey,

I got your message, "Chin up, keep smiling," to day.
Honestly, that's not what I want to hear, so it helps. Which is the
weirdest thing ever? !

I tried not to think of you today, which is like trying not
to think about a purple horse. So I try to think of you as just a
friend, which you are, but so much more. I only allow the friend
part, and fight like hell to keep out the rest.

It wears me out, this game I play.
Keeping you far away.
Yet, unless I do I could lose,
and I don't do self abuse.
This gift we have, is it done?
Is your freedom the battle won?
I know not what tomorrow brings
'Cept fore dawn the sparrow sings.

No, my Dearest, I smile not. except at Lotto fantasies, when I could lay priceless, meaningless trinkets at your feet. We both know where the real treasure lies; in each other and what is between us. Now you must work for your freedom, and I feel helpless. Like it's your show and I am not allowed to attend. Contrary to my "normal" reactions, it is best I don't. Yet the normal reactions are there. So, my Dearest, the smile is more of a grief grimace and it will return when you do.
I love you,
X

12/10/93 11 AM

Dearest Donna,
I started rereading the letters today. As I read what I have written I see more of why falling in love with you is so damn difficult. Part of this is simply not natural. My love for you is the most natural thing that has ever happened to me. Your being married is what is unnatural. No, that's not right. Being married is, or can be wonderful. My falling in love with you **while you are still married** is what is unnatural. Even though in many respects, all you have is a piece of paper, we both honor it as a barrier to our progress. Without the honor, there would be no progress. So, falling deeply in love with a married woman is placing myself in Catch 22, a trick bag only your freedom can get us out of.
I love you,
X

11:45 PM
Dearest Donna,
I have never loved or desired like this before. Were it I knew the words to describe what this is like, knowing what you go through every time he is around. God, woman! I know you are strong. It just seems a shame to waste your strength on this needless self defence. Needless because there must be other options. I have no idea what they are except come here, and that too has its price.

Oh, I want to jump in, and this restraint is exhausting.
It's worse than aerobics. When you are free, my Precious, then I
will breathe fresh life.
Love,
X

12/11/93 Midnight

Dearest Donna,

I reread more letters today. Sometimes it's pretty painful
stuff. I always feel light with you; sometimes it lasts quite a
while. Then I realized where you are and I feel badly for you.
Then I become aware you are not with me and I feel badly for
me. (Ladies before gentlemen.)

I sometimes wonder when the us will be, then if the us
will be. Every few days when we talk, it is a breath of air for a
drowning man. Yet when we do, it de-focuses you from the
steps you have to take. It would be nice to will the Lotto,
drawbacks and all. It would be great at first.

Either Kafka or Nietzsche says what doesn't kill us,
makes us stronger, whoever. I'll either be dead or damn near as
strong as you are. It's pretty weird, really. We pretty much have
the same value systems, fairly similar goals, similar wants (each
other) yet you are there and I am here. And I know you have to
be. Even with the Lotto, we could simply be closer for a while.

Oh, my Precious One, I want to court you, maybe for the
rest of my life. Flowers, and song and dance and poems of one
love, our love. Poems of passion, and unity and desire finally
slaked. Poems of bonding and our nakedness before each other,
before and after. Poems of bathing together the sacred bath, and
poems of shower fun. Poems of laughter and joy. Poems of
children playing and family song. Poems of sleazy barrooms and
fancy balls and poems of tears and sorrow and anguish as we live
life to its fullest with all its ups and downs.

I love you as surely as the sun will rise this morning with
a depth beyond my comprehension and I can comprehend the
distance to the sun in inches, the distance to Pluto at oppositional

perigee in millimeters. I can comprehend the last cardinal number, Aleph sub null, but this is beyond me. There is a frightening beauty in being here, and the thought of your loss is the essence of fear, the lights go out and poetry dies. Will you hold my hand?

I love you,

X

12/12/93 8 AM

Dearest Donna,

Funny thing happened. The sun rose. By gollies, I guess I love you. I'm going to get you roses today. There is so much of me bottled up, I will explode if I cannot give you a small token. You may not be able to accept them. He may be there. You may not be there. All I can do is try. If you are not there, then I will leave them in the door tomorrow. Wouldn't it be nice could I walk up to your door, knock and be asked to enter? Sit for a moment or two while you took care of last minute things and primping, then we left for an evening out? A light dinner, movie, dancing? The simple, normal wants of life. A good night kiss. Then, would we be able to leave each other? It would be so wondrously different.

Just thoughts of you, as always.

I love you,

X

3:30 PM - Precious, Dearest Donna,

I saw you and gave you the roses, When we hugged, I felt your heart beating with mine in love's rhythm. We kissed and it was just so right. God, I love you! When we talked, you said my hugs were like warm caramel flowing over ice cream. My Dearest, you are the poet! I love you. I'm glad you think I'm easy to love too. You and I are just so natural with each other. I trust you. I feel good with you. I feel joy with you.

Well, tomorrow I will try hugging my pillow, pretending it is you and I will look for your face in the sunrise. Yes, Precious One, I love all of you. For being so small, there is so

much of you to love. I think it will take me a lifetime. 'What a
Journey!

Precious, I know now how much you love me. Thank
you. I feel like it is as much as I love you and both are beyond
me. About all we will be able to give each other for Christmas is
our love for each other. What a precious gift! Soon, we can tell
the world, Won't they be lucky to see us together?

I am so filled with your love. What a gift! I am
delighted to hear you are going to wait on the Boss. Though you
probably won't be over here until the end of January, its OK.
Knowing you love me is all I need. I'd rather have you here
yesterday, or a year ago.

You once said all you ever wanted was to be loved. You
are. I do. Me too. Part of me wonders why I was so stupid for
so long. The other part says, you weren't ready yet, and neither
was I. You told me today of your attempted rape when you were
13. Wow! I guess you were tough! Going back and talking that
guy into being your sex partner until you had an orgasm, then
dumping him. Ugg! That's cold! I'm glad you've changed.
God's timing is great!
I love you.
X

9 PM
Hi Honey,

I had my barbecued chicken, yellow rice and the most
wonderful nap. I think next I'll whip up some of my addictive
spaghetti sauce, and eat spaghetti for a while. My old friend Paul
once told me if the DEA ever got hold of it, I'd be in a heap of
trouble. Best compliment I ever had on my cooking. Paul was
just a little fellow, but he would put away two huge plates.

So many things I want to tell you. They come into my
head and are pushed away by other thoughts, which are in turn
are pushed away, but they are all the same I love you's just said
differently. It was funny today when you said you'd heard a lot
of words from different guys - as beautiful as you are, I can
believe it. Then I told you I had 90 pages of them. Oh well.

Warm caramel flowing on ice cream. I'm sitting here
grinning, a wrap around ear splitter. You are so much fun. What

is it going to be like when you aren't looking over your shoulder?
When you are free? Will you glow more than you do now? You
are so radiant.

The biggest event for me today was asking you to be my
beloved. And your saying you were, I was, we are. Beloved is
so powerful:

MY BELOVED

Thou art my beloved on whom
Rain falls gently to clean her skin,
Sun shines warmly, warming within.
The wind blows softly, caressing her face,
Grass cushions her feet as she walks with grace.
My beloved shines like a beacon fixed,
Hair blowing gently, eyes softly relax.
I dream of her in diaphanous white,
Sliding to the floor, to spend first night.
The oneness upon us soon to be
And she shan't be her and I not me.
Yet we are the same, only more than one
As children don't dream of wonders to come.

Wow! I love you.
X

5 PM
Dearest Donna,

For some reason, I am very secure in your love. The sun
came up this morning. Thinking of you next to me . . . well, the
pillow didn't cut it. Thank you, my beloved, for your gift. I will
always honor it.

It's funny. I'm neither secure nor insecure about our
future. I no longer even feel a need for expectations. Knowing
you love me is pretty filling. Do I want us to grow together? Of
course. My desires have remained the same. I no longer expect
you to fill them. I just like being loved by you. I love loving
you. I feel wonderful, except I feel for you in your predicament.
I also admire you for the steps you are taking to try and get out of
it. You are one tough little gal!

82

I was thinking earlier today about business trips with you. Years ago, I heard taking your wife on a business trip was like taking a sandwich to a banquet. Regardless of the women's beauty around there, taking you would be much more like taking Chateaubriand to a potluck dinner!

I smile every time I think of warm caramel flowing on ice cream. When do I get to eat the sundae? Honey, I feel so much lighter now. Thank you. I love you, my beloved.
X

7 PM
My Beloved,

The sun was shining beyond the clouds. The day was grey until I heard your voice on the answering machine. I screwed up and forgot to save your voice after the 5th or 6th time I played it yesterday. Then Sam called and erased it.

You know I want to hear about your dream. I called today to tell you how grey it was and Ruth answered and said you were ill. You probably need some of my chicken soup, laden with TLC. Tomorrow I have to take some to an agent who sends us work.

You know how I value your ability to dream, and your takes on them. You have done well with them in the past. I believe you following the insight obtained from them is one of your strong points. I say all this without knowing if or how it may involve me. I hope it does and it is what I would think of as good news. Whether or not, I will support your following it.

I may do so kicking and screaming if it is bad news for me. I will do everything in my power to try and turn it to my favor, all the while recognizing the futility of arguing with the Source. Jacob tried it and walked with a limp the rest of his life. A limp is a small price to pay to have you with me.

So, My Beloved, tell me your dream. I have the feeling it is good news for us. I love you so much, and wish you were with me right now to share your dream when it was fresh, like when you woke up. I will love giving you an early good morning hug.
Love,
X

12/16/93 8 PM

Beloved Donna,

This morning I decided I was completely insane, absolutely mad, totally bonkers. You have four, count them; one two, three, four lovely children and I don't care. I actually like the idea. I am mad! Worse, today I slipped into a jewelry store and looked at rings in your size. I am mad!

I am also a little sad. Christmas and you won't be here. Oh, you will be in my heart, but not my arms. You will be in my thoughts, but not my house. You will be in my prayers, but not my bed. As I told you when we spoke last, I trust you to know exactly when the time is right for us. We will have it right. I don't really like the wait, but I know you will be worth it.
I love you,
X

12/17/93 9 AM

Beloved Donna,

The grey skies drizzle tears of sadness for our apartness, yet the sun shines in my heart. My infamous spaghetti sauce will not meet my high standards in this batch. It has been years since I made it last and I screwed up with the sausage. It will work, but it's not the best. It was on all night and may be ready by this evening.

I wanted to work today, but the rain . . . so, I will get busy with other things. I just wanted to let you know I am thinking about you always.
Love,
X

8 PM
My Beloved,

You called. Too brief our words, yet so powerful: I love you and we are in each other's heart. You started to say you wanted to do something, but we were interrupted by someone's arrival. And I sit and wait. Now, I must wait again for you to

tell me what it is you propose, and tell me again you love me so
your love makes me the bright star worthy to accompany you on
our journey, as mine does for you.
I love you,
X

12/22/93 7 PM

Dearest Beloved Donna,

    I apologize for not writing - doesn't mean I'm not
thinking of you. It was wonderful to talk with you last Monday.
I keep losing your phone messages and I'm so glad you keep
replenishing them. Glad to hear about your sister, though it was
a monologue, rather than a conversation.

    I finally got the car. It's a lot nicer than the other one,
but it needs a lot of cleaning and cosmetic work. I burned dinner.
The place is full of smoke. The spaghetti sauce. I've been so
tired lately, instead of turning the burner down, I turned another
one on to low. I put the sauce on high, briefly I thought, to take
the chill out of the Dutch Oven. Oh well. Burger King.

    I really need to confront my fears with you - my fear
about us. The one I told you about Monday paralyzing me
Sunday. I know as soon as I see you and hold you and talk with
you about it, it will go away. It needs to be confronted. But I
don't want to burden you with it, I want to share it with you.

    Honey, it's about sex. Things with you are so different. I
like sex. A lot. There were a few times when I didn't really care
about my partner, as long as I got my rocks off. But most of the
time my ego satisfaction came from pleasing a woman in the
fullest. With you it will be different. Don't worry, You will be
pleasured before we start. It's just I anticipate a sacred nature to
the act with which I never have dealt consciously, before you.
This will be, as you are, very, very special. Part of me wants to
treat you as other women, but you are not other women. You are
a woman I love with a depth and breadth never before felt. And
you love me as well! What I feel from you is colossal. And you
hold back!

There is something wrong with this picture. The wrongness comes from my never seeing it before, never even imagining it, and being caught up in it like a bait fish too near Niagara Falls. The current is strong. Too strong. I am being swept away to a beautiful land I knew not of. So what happens when we get naked? It's not you. You are certainly no Mary-Madonna. It is the power of what is between us. There! I said it. I confronted it. Now I need to do this with you. Of course, there are a lot of things I need to do with you. I would list them, but I have only two or three dozen pads of paper left.

The sauce was ruined. Garbage disposal time. I hope the pot is OK? Curing it again is such a pain. BK time. I love you more than I can say.

X

12/23/93 9:30 PM

My Beloved Donna,

I have survived aloneness many Christmases now. I will survive this one too, though the degree of difficulty has multiplied. Like from a front dive layout off the one meter board to a double twisting reverse three and a half from the three-meter board. Knowing you are in my heart, and I in yours, helps. Yet my arms and bed are empty. I went to a gathering at Tiffany's tonight. Pigged out on the hors d'oeuvres and came home early. Tired. I've been exhausted lately. I need a hug. I need your touch and nourishment. Why you? Because you love me, as I love you: deeply, passionately, fully. It is scary. Funny too. I am either very courageous or very foolish. I have been both before and couldn't tell which was which until much later. The one thing I know is fools walk in where angels fear to tread. Since you walk with angels, I am in good company. I love you, my Beloved.

X

12/24/93 9 PM

Merry Christmas My Beloved,

I'm so glad you dropped by today. I never did get my nap, but the car looks good. I finally finished around 6:30, washed all the towels, ate some Chinese and took a shower.

Are you great! I love snuggling with you. I'm delighted we can do things you've never done before. I want to groom you too, just brush your hair and touch you. All this is still to quick, although this visit was a little longer and much better! Honey, you have made my Christmas. I still wish you were here or, I wish you were still here.

I am tired - again - these 13 hour days are beginning to get to me. Funny, were it summer I would not have had to work as fast and hard. It would have been light longer. I'll finish the windows tomorrow before breakfast and that will be it.

THE PROMISE SONNET

Today was a promise of things to be.
Yesterday's gone and left way behind
Tomorrow's a promise for you and me.
Why can't I get you off my mind?
Your beauty permeates my heart and soul
Your words of wisdom and love as well
Your ancient spirit helps to make me whole
Repeated by me 'cause I love to tell
I'll share you with world and heav'n between
I want to hold fast and wake next to you
I'll shout from the roof you are my Queen.
Would you like my name? You can have it too.
Tomorrow's a promise for you and me.
Today was a promise of things to be.

I love you,
X

12/25/93 6 PM

Beloved Donna,
		Merry Christmas, Dearest One. I washed those scuzzy sweats I wore when you came yesterday and slept in them last night. I think I'll sleep in them again tonight. I'd rather sleep in you, but I'll have to wait on that, for a while. I just fixed a cup of cocoa, and was thinking how wonderful it would be were you here to share it. Snuggling, sipping hot chocolate. Ooooh!
		I pretty much finished the car today, as much as I can. Tomorrow, after church, I'll get some flat or semi-gloss paint for the windshield trim, and X Jr. gave me some high gloss for the wipers. Then it will be as done as it's going to get until some money comes in. I'll also try fixing the visor - see if JB Weld works on pot metal.
(Later)   One chocolate was good; two were better

> *The butterfly spread her wings*
> *The wind whistles and the flower sings*
> *The wind died and went away*
> *But he came back another day.*

I love you,
X

12/26/93 10 PM

Hi Honey,
		Boy! Am I tired! Missed Church. Got paint. Painted the wipers and window trim on the car. I have to shim the visor. Did a laundry and two weeks ironing. Cooked a chicken for soup. New brand. Tough. That's enough, except one of the reasons I don't like winter is having to iron all those long sleeve shirts.
		I am still thrilled about your visit. It was so wonderful seeing you and holding you and especially . . . I enjoyed you

immensely. It was such a surprise! I mean, I hardly ever think
about you (Ho Ho) and there you were. Well you didn't get to
knock me over in the driveway. I remembered what you said and
tried to preempt you by carrying you up to the house. Great
excuse to hold you.

I can still taste your kisses. The memory of your body
next to me, and your sitting in my lap in the chair, all those
things. You simply feel so natural to be with. Like it's supposed
to be. Soon we can really be with each other. Thank you for
being.
I love you.
X

12/28/93 9 PM

Dearest Donna,

Your message yesterday said you had a small anxiety
attack, were going home, and would call today. You didn't. I
worry about you. I could blow up, get angry and your not calling
(loss of reasonable expectation) and all the normal stuff. But, I
know you. I know you love me and would call if you could.
That's what worries me! You are so precious to me. I know it's
rough on you. I talk about what I do; fix the car, laundry, cook,
iron, ya de da de da. I'm doing for one and you do for six, plus
work plus, plus, plus.

Anyway, my precious, I simply want to share with you
who I am, what I do and what I feel. I do this vulnerability thing
so you will do it with me. We know pretty much each other's
morals, desires, values, and we have resolved the very important
"inny" or "outy" issue regarding paper on rolls. There is so much
more about you I could love, if I only knew.

I feel very comfortable with you. I trust you. I guess
this is why I worry when you didn't call today. Are you still at
the house, not feeling well?   Did you have to go to the hospital?
Was there not a free moment at work? I'd prefer the latter. At
least you'd be relatively all right.

Precious papillon, my petite butterfly with beautiful wing
Close to my body warm, my heart and soul vibrate and sing.
With a universal harmony and theme for lovers two
Holding, kissing caressing, my fingers slide smoothly over you
.

I'm less tired than previously. I think I shut some things out that were stressing me. Regardless, tomorrow is another early day so I'll close for now, always thinking of you.
Love,
X

12/29/93

My Beloved,
      It relieved me to hear from you today and you were OK. I'm not used to this! I'm not used to being in love with a married woman. I'm not use to your anxiety attacks. So I sit and wait and worry and wait . . . I hope you come again Friday.
I love you.
X

2:30 PM
Hi Honey,
      All the stuff is done and I can sit with you for a minute. It will be longer than a minute, and I might take a lunch break pretty soon. Anyway, I'm glad you know how much I love you. Someday, maybe you can explain it to me. I'm glad I can feel so much passion with you in my life. I'm so damn intellectual . . . Maybe that is why I have to make a list.
      First let me apologize for asking about your actions the other day. I want you to know I appreciate you. Let me tell you what I think they are in addition to raising six kids, working full time and living in a clusterbleep, and you can tell me if I'm wrong. You are getting rid of the baggage so many women carry with them. This is not easy. It takes a lot of work and time. My problem is I can't see it. You keep me locked away, not even talking on a regular basis, it is difficult for me to appreciate how hard you are working. I know you are, but I keep forgetting it. I'll trust you.

On top of that, you are doing this with a damn near uncontrollable desire for me, like when your hands were jerking back and forth the day you took your rings off. That's work! So let me get to the list.

1. I've kissed a girl, or six, in my day, but never have their lips swollen with desire as do yours. Wow!

2. You are prettier than a speckled puppy. That by itself is no big deal. There are millions of pretty girls out there. Your real beauty comes from the inside, narrowing the field a lot. (When I see a pretty package, I like to open it up and see what's inside.)

3. For me, you are a walking aphrodisiac. The ultimate. What is really weird for me is I get turned on by thinking about how much I love you, without any erotic thoughts at all! That's weird! I'm just sitting around, thinking about what a wonderful human being you are, and Oops! Look at that!

That's a good start on *eros*. Let's go to *agape*.

1. I admire your relationship with The Boss. I want to learn more about it. I talk to Him a lot, and seldom listen, except when it came to you, and a few other times. You not only listen, you act on what you hear. I need more of this in my life.

2. You consistently remind me about Him, and who is really in control of our lives (neither of us). I need the reminder.

3. In some areas, I think you are a little wacky, and perhaps off base. I'll call you on them when we have time. Right now, my limited moments with you are too precious to waste on some involved theological discussion. Who knows? I may be wrong and have the opportunity to learn something.

4. You are far more aware of your spirit self than am I of mine. Being aware of your spiritual essence is the definition of spirituality. I laugh at myself when I think of how hard I worked to get "more spiritual." It finally dawned on me I was as spiritual as I was ever going to get, because that is the way The Boss created me.

5. Your commitment to the Institution of Marriage. A lot of folks have ideas on what marriage is supposed to be for their partner, but the rules for *them* are a little different. I have mixed feelings about us, but a lot of that is nothing but hormones yelling. The rules don't care about hormones.

You mentioned emotional adultery. I'm sorry. We've done it. You told me you wouldn't allow yourself to go there in your head. Nevertheless, you know with every fiber, you have somewhere to go when your "marriage" fails. The first time you returned my kiss was adulterous. The flip side of the coin is it was not until after you shared with me the deceit perpetrated on you, this happened.

When you long for me to hold you, as I want to, and touch your face and caress you, and stroke your hair, Honey, that is adultery, IF you are married. It is what is deep in our heart that counts, at least according to Matthew. You don't have to go there with your head. You are not alone. It takes two. I am guilty as well. Our justification does not count. The rules don't care. By the same token, Ralph "set you aside" in favor of crack. According to Deut., it was his duty to give you "a bill of divorcement." I don't know. We're just human beings doing the best we can with a lot of love in our hearts. God is the judge. Not you or me. Everybody I know trying to argue or bargain with The Boss lost. I don't know where that leaves us, but I fully intend to keep going.

I want to go to *philos* now.

1. I love laughing with you. We have a similar sense of humor, and seem to appreciate the same things.

2. Part of *philos*, brotherly love, deep friendship, is recognizing who and what we are. You recognize you are currently a "married" woman - I mentally annulled your marriage when you told me of his deceit, but I'm not married, you are - and in spite of the powerful desire I feel from you (and I have for you) you have locked me away. You do this simply so the mirror won't shame you when you brush your teeth. I believe this is integrity. I like that. (A lot of times I don't)

3. You are clearing away the wreckage of the past to leave free. Where ever you go, whom ever you wind up with (me?) you will not drag any excess baggage with you. You are going only with your wonderful self. I like that. I just forget it takes time.

4. Your transparency. (I took a break for PB&J.) You are so easy to read, most of the time I, Mr. Oblivious, know what is going on. I can hear it in your voice over the phone.

5. Your name. You value your name. So do I. Maybe
that is a part of integrity.

6. I believe you will make a good partner. You have
skills in areas I do not have. You have an attitude of getting with
it, regardless of the fates. If the stuff hits the fan, you have the
fortitude to get up and go right on.

Wow! I'm glad I made this list. I didn't know how much
philos was there! I know there is a lot more *agape* (and *eros*) but
I can't bring the *agape* to surface and I'd rather demonstrate the
eros.

Closing this off for now, the most comforting thing you
said to me in our conversation is you still consider me as husband
material. The way you said it, as if there were no question about
it, relieved a lot of my anxiety. Springs unwound. Ahhhh!
Thank you. Again, I want to let you know I appreciate these
unseen efforts. And I feel much better as a British engineer
listing and categorizing the list. Satisfies my intellectual side.
I've been so damn passionate, one would think I was Irish!
I love you.
X

12/31/93 8:30 PM

Dearest Donna,

Happy New Year. Last week you shared your sadness
with me on the loss of your marriage. I told you it was normal
and healthy to feel this. I was so happy you shared this with me,
and happy you were dealing with your feelings. This was such
positive news. That was then and this is now. Now I'm sad.

Precious one, I am sad we have not talked and shared
with each other. I am sad I did not see you today. I am sad over
a week of empty arms. I keep grieving for you. And then, as a
miracle, you call or show up at my door. We talk, between hugs
and kisses, and everything is OK again.

This has to be tough on you too. You have to live under
the same roof with someone who isn't who you thought he was. I
would like to have you validate this thought; this is tough on you.
Then there's me, and you as my beloved, and you still must hide
this. Just a thought: am I who you think I am?

This is bittersweet sadness. I wonder if you are going out for show tonight, what is going on with and in you? Are you going up to West Palm and watch them blow up the building? About the only thing I don't wonder about is your love. I do wonder when you will be able to show it freely. Even to me again.

This, once called "pining" is the down side of loving a "married" woman. Melancholia. Depression. Sadness. Sorrow. All to be lifted only to return while I wait at my end and you at yours. Why do we marry? What are our expectations from the union? We have talked about this in great depth, and have yet to scratch the surface. I must tell you, you fulfill the common masculine answers of lust and trophy hunting. You are the most desirable and beautiful woman I have ever known. (Jane Seymour, eat your heart out! A few others too.) Yes my Dearest, you easily and readily fill those two criteria. Another reason is money. (Ho Ho.) I'm glad we're both broke dollar wise. Yet we are so rich in other ways, the money will come. And you, you are the richest of us all. We both have wealth beyond our wallets. So, let us marry for wealth, rather than money.

I wish you were here with me now. Since there is a probability of .99 (nothing is certain) you will be with me next year, let it be tomorrow.
I love you.
X

1/2/94

Dearest Donna,

My sadness abated and resentment moved in. I'm a little ticked I haven't heard from you, particularly after the intimacy we shared last week. Are you angry with me? Are you ashamed? What's going on?

I feel like a boss diddled secretary, where he keeps promising to divorce his wife to marry her and it never happens. If you have made your decision to file and leave, then do it. If things have changed, then let me know. I'm really easy. You have never lied to me. So whatever you tell me, I generally accept. All I've asked is you tell me.

I'm no longer in the way between you and him. You made your decision to leave because of his abuse and deceit and your self respect. The longer you stay, the more difficult it becomes for you to leave. I have patience, but it needs padding. Is this what I will look forward to? Our relationship is built on our communication. When you stop talking, I can't listen. I find it hard to believe you cannot find time to pick up the phone and leave me a message.

Is there such a thing as caring too much? If there is, I guess I do. And I care for me too as I wander this limbo land - the purgatory of my mind. We keep hearing all about women in this predicament. I wonder how many men fall into this trap?

THE TRAP
The trap cares not which gender it snares
It laughs with each victim fresh.
Its rose covered entrance beckons with love
Till the thorns rip and tear the flesh.

What doesn't kill us makes us stronger. I will survive. So will you. I'd just like it to be together. Anger does not diminish my love; it just gets in the way.
I love you.
X

1/3/94 6 PM

Dearest Donna,

Well, there's the rub! We just got off the phone. So, he's being a good boy now. It seems different to you. You don't know what to do. Well, as long as you are with him, I don't stand a chance!

I thought when you took your rings off, that was it. On or off, you go home to him. That's the rub. The futility! Nothing can ever happen between us to develop the power of this our love, of what we have, while you are there.

While you are there, you are going to keep getting what you always received: abuse, nice, abuse, nice, etc. The pattern will continue. I think you are too good for that. Obviously, you don't. Frankly, I think you deserve better, maybe even better than me. I've been patient since the first day I saw you. In August, it was November, then early January, now . . .? I am sorry. No, I'll give it one more try when we speak again Friday. I will ask you not to turn your nose up at this gift. To me, this is a sin. Not one you pay for in Hell, but one you pay for here.

Precious one, maybe we don't make it. It's not important. What is important, to me at any rate, is you see the futility of the game you are in and get out! Giving us a try is next. If nothing else, I can show you another way, if you want it. Oh yes, you only get one bath partner. Choose wisely.

I love you and what you have shown me.

X

1/4/94

Dear Donna,

Thanks for the message. It's so nice to be loved "for who I am." It is extremely flattering to be told I am loved and desired by one as beautiful as you are. Holding you and loving you brought great pleasure, joy and happiness into my life, but I can go no further.

I feel really stupid. The bottom line is every night you go home to him. You spend time with him. You talk with him. You went out New Year's Eve with him. I may have an hour a week on the phone with you, if that. As a friend pointed out, possession is nine tenths of the law. You are in his possession.

Dearest one, love is a feeling complemented with action. Where is and has been your action? My action is these letters, waiting for you to call - waiting is an action, calling you when I dared, preparing a business plan for you so you could be independent - even from me, telling my friends and children about you. The biggest action you have taken, other than my Christmas present, was the removal of your rings. I thought that was it. It is a symbol obviously having more significance to me than you. It was because of this I could accept your gift. Now

you tell me you were really angry? I assume, now that he is a
nice guy again, eventually they will go back on.

Donna, I deserve more. I would rather have nothing than
this. I'm used to nothing. Being jerked around like this sucks!
You are not deliberately doing it to me. It is happening. He's
jerking you around and I'm on the end of the whip. For the most
part, I've been alone the many years since my divorce and I like
my company. I would have liked yours too, but all of it. You
must do what you must do, but until you leave him and are
divorced, it will be without me. It may be without me even then.

Am I sad and hurt? Yes. I am sad for a lot of reasons.
First, I feel what is between us is a powerful gift, one to be
cherished and honored. I've done that. Have you? I don't think
so, Not now. Had I looked, I probably wouldn't have earlier, but
I've told you many times in some areas of my life, I'm not too
swift.

I'm sad I let my ego override my common sense. It was
wonderful being loved by you. You are beautiful, in so many
ways strong and courageous, and very different is a super special
way. Yet, I believed you were going to leave him, in spite of
what I have seen to the contrary. Back to the 3%; 97% of abused
women either return to the same man or the same man with a
different name. I thought you were one of the 3%. Maybe you're
not. Let's face it. You went from one abusive marriage into
another, this one compounded with drugs and deceit, yet you
stay. I also thought my love for you, this demonstration, would
show you an alternative lifestyle more attractive to you. I was
wrong.

I am sad you have decided to stay with him, for another
five minutes, or day or month or however long it is. When it
came to you, what little "smarts" I had, went out the window.
You are there with him, not here with me. Oh, I may be in your
heart, but you are not in my arms. The actions you take speak
louder than the words you say and I must listen to your actions. I
have to think you could have occasionally sent a card, or called
more often. I bought and chewed upon what you were trying to
do, but it has soured in my stomach. I have understood, but my
understanding is confused, as am I.

Am I angry with you? Heavens no! I know you love me in a vacillating sort of way. I know you have the capacity for great love. You deserved to be loved. Just as an observer, it distresses me to see you waste it on him, you and millions of others of women. But it is your choice. I certainly can't change them; I can't change you.

Oh. Those special towels I bought and saved for our shower and our bath, I used last night. I forgot to take the regular towels out of the dryer. I just said, "to hell with it." I may even throw them away. They are a reminder of what could have been, and I don't want to live there. Life is too precious to spend being an unwilling and unrewarded participant in The Game. Beside, you are too tough an act to follow, and you should know me well enough by now to know I will not settle!

I can't help you anymore. I can't help loving you any less. Since you will not choose, I must. Goodbye, Sweet Love.
X

1/9/94 9 PM

Dearest Donna
Having to tell you good bye is the most painful loss. My Mother's death was easier. The sweet words from your sweet lips are echoing "I'm coming to you - greatest lover and we haven't done anything yet - I love you - I'm in love with you - you're a little piece of heaven - you're a breath of fresh air." These words from you mean so much to me. Others could use them with no effect. Coming from you, they were solid nourishment for a starving soul.

I don't know anything now. I can't click off and on at will. Part of me wants to die. Part of me wishes you were here to kiss the tears from my eyes and face. At least I could then see the paper on which I write. I have missed you before, but now, part of my soul is gone. You filled it with your love. A large balloon has burst and all remaining is but flaccid rubber, a shell of what once was, to be cast into the garbage like the rest of over used goods.

I will heal. The jagged edges of the balloon will come together, and knit leaving a scar. Scars are good. They form when the healing is complete. I never knew it would be this painful You carried me to new heights of joy. Now your absence drops me to depths I have not seen, and must decompress from. It is not your absence, rather my decision to tell you good bye. You are not responsible for my behavior or the consequences I must bear from it. I am.

When you changed your mind about filing when you told me you would, I thought it was more than I could bear; wait again. The good news is I am now really aware of how much, how deeply I love you, and how much I value you. This is totally unexpected. Duh ! . . . Denial can be a friend one moment and an enemy the next. One would say these emotions blind sided me. The truth is I put the blinders up so I would not see it coming. I didn't.

I wonder if I will write to you forever, like John Wayne on the Yangtze River talked to his imaginary girl friend. It kept him from "becoming emotionally involved." (PC for falling in love.)

Were you and I other than who we are . . . Maybe I can will a psychosis into a parallel universe where we are other than who we are. There, these feeling for you do not exist. "Feelings!" What a trite word. The proper word is love. Total, honest, committed - maybe committable - love!

Falling in love and divorce both breed their own form of insanity. I prefer the former. Donna, I was placing expectations again. I believe you were helping. I expected you to file when you said you would. Granted, I asked for that date. You said you would and you didn't. The explanation? The Boss hadn't told you to. I thought He had. The date was an afterthought. These errors in communication will occur when we don't talk much.

It's over now. The pain abates. Reason returns. I still love you so much. I hope someday . . . well . . . maybe not.
Love,
X

VOICES

In pre-dawn silence
there are voices.
Perhaps the radio
left on too low,
or the TV
in the other room.
I listen,
muffled voices.
I strain to hear
listen,
to the voices.

Coffee driven tintinitis
crickets, critters
chirping provide
high frequency overtones
for refrigerator's rumble
as white noise warm air rustles
in long shiny boxes.
Voices.

Voices saying...

Voices saying... "Alone."

8/28/94 8:15 PM

Dear Donna,

It was good to see you today, though instantly I knew things were not well with you. It's nice to know you and be able to read you. I could have said, "I told you so, and I told you so over a year ago." You knew it and you knew it then, so why bother? I'm really sorry you all went into business together. I am glad you said you'd call. Why the hell am I still writing to you? Force of habit I guess.

I'll bring you up to date when you call. Basically I moped around for a couple of months, lamenting what could have been, but what wasn't gonna be for us. I met a young lady and did something unusual. I took a risk and asked her out for coffee. We went and it was a wonderful evening.

We started dating, and things were progressing in, I guess, the typical jerky fashion. I must admit to comparing her with you in a way where she compared favorably. Yet, there was something missing. I cared for her very deeply, yet when I said, "I love you," it was the old 3/4 kind; the kind I got married and divorced twice with, not the 100% kind I felt with you. You really screwed me up, kid.

Anyway, I guess she knew it and began behaving in a way unacceptable to me, so we parted on friendly terms. Strange, there was concern for her, but little of the moping around. I felt OK either way.

I guess something still lingers for you. I know if there is anything I can do to help you extricate yourself, I will if you want me to. Boy! Is that hesitant! Anyway, I'll look for your call, and try not to glue myself to the phone as I once did, waiting for the sound of your voice.
Love,
X

8/31/94 8 PM

Dear Donna,

You shocked me by your phone call today. No, not about the part where Ralph was back on crack and he had a couple of girl friends on the side. First, he never got off to get back on. That only happens in a locked treatment center, and then not all the time. The girl friends are the enablers you won't be for him. You just give him cover; pretty wife, good church girl, nice kids, who would think he's an addict? Not to mention the money you bring in to support his habit. That is not news to me.

What upset me was your telling me my former girl friend called you and accused you of "fucking her boy friend all last year." For a moment, I pleasantly thought about it, wishing it were true. Then it hit me. She wouldn't do that. She couldn't do that.

The only thing ringing true was the use of the word, "boy friend." We made it a big deal. I liked it. You and I were never boy/girl friends. We could not act openly. She and I could, and it was neat. I was proud to be her "boy friend." It was a new experience.

Next, she knew about you as, "a married woman I was once in love with, but who decided to stay with her husband, so I left." This is true. I told her about the book and someday I'd let her read it. I can't remember whether or not I told her all we ever had together were a few moments at a time in public. Whatever I told her, it was the truth. Granted, I did not tell her about the depth of our feelings or desire. There was no need, and I was trying to get on with my life.

In some ways, she was a little wild and crazy, but she had way too much class to pull a stunt like that. Even if she did, she doesn't know your name, much less your phone number. So, I say, "couldn't." The only thing I can think of is if your phone number is on the deposit slip - the one you used to leave me the note I saved. I don't know how. I locked it away, as I tried to lock you away. I'll check and get back to you.
Love,
X

9/3/94 10 PM

Dearest Donna,

I'm glad we talked today and each of us figured things out. You figured out it would take you about three weeks to leave Ralph, and I finally figured out where I hid the folder with all your letters. Since your number is not on the deposit slip, and it is not listed, she didn't get it. Well, she's a smart cookie, and could have, but not likely. I'm glad we figured out it was probably one of Ralph's stoned girl friends who didn't know he was married. Based on what you've told me about him it still wasn't very true. I mean, three or four times doesn't constitute "all year." Oh well.

Honey, I am so happy for you and for us. I feel a sense of hope for us I haven't felt in a long, long time.
Love,
X

9/17/94 8:15 PM

Dearest Donna,

It seems to me you are going to a lot of trouble to get the business in your name. It is still a "marital asset." I know how important it is to you to own your own business. And, you are good at it. But, Honey,. . . I just don't know. I would strongly suggest you get legal advice on this matter. You can open your own business later. I've always made money for others. I would love to make it for you too. It would be a lot of fun for me. I love telling people how wonderful you are!

Like I told you, if this is what you want, I'll check around and see how I can help, Fat Lips. (I see they still swell.)
Love,
X

10/3/94 4 PM
 Dear Donna,
        Well, here we are again. Your "three weeks" has come
and gone and you are still working on your "dots and dittles." I
understand you only have a limited amount of time to do these
things, and they do take time.
        I know how you feel about marriage and now it's over for
you. There are no physical, emotional, or spiritual ties. You did
a wonderful job of doing every thing in your power to make it
work. There is nothing holding you now. Now it is done.
Unfortunately, the law says, "It ain't over till the fat lady sings,"
some Judge being the fat lady. Putting everything in your name
may give you all the responsibility for debt, while he steals you
blind. I don't know. Please get some legal advice.
        In the meantime, I'll start looking for contractors so you
can sub out work and increase sales. Tiffany is having her house
painted soon. I'll ask her to make discrete inquires.
        You are really too much. I mean, I wrote you a book of
love letters and poetry and got nowhere. Today, I tell you I do
windows and you pop out with the nicest "I love you" I've heard
in a long time. Go figure!
Love,
X

10/17/94 8 PM

Dearest Donna,
        I'm glad you put your foot in the fire and stirred things
up. Telling Ralph he was "going to have to get a side job
because the business wouldn't support his habit and girl friends"
was cool! I'm proud of you for finally standing up and
confronting the issue. Just be careful. The most important thing
in his life is his addiction. Generally speaking, an addict will do
whatever it takes to remove anything standing between him and
his addiction.
        As long as I have a home, you and the kids are welcome.
It will be crowded, but it will be safe.
Love,
X

10/18/94 4:30 PM

Oh Honey!
I feel so badly about my call to you today. I'm so sorry.
Tiffany blabbed everything to those contractors; drugs, divorce,
and gave them your name! They said Ralph was wonderful and
not nice things about you. I had to warn you. If, or when Ralph
finds out, you and the kids could be in danger.
I can't say any more now.
X

10/20/94 7:30 AM

Dearest Donna,
As you need my affirmation, I now need yours. You
know I love you beyond my comprehension;   As King David felt
like a worm in one of his early Psalms, unworthy of God's love
and mercy, do I also feel unworthy of yours. I can say, "I
grievously erred," or "I screwed-up big time," either way I feel
badly.
Thank you for reminding me things occur in God's time,
not ours. This must be the way it is supposed to be. I was so
glad to hear you voice this morning, glad you are OK and the
weapons are hidden. This is but another example of your contact
with The Boss, the source of your strength and direction. I am
honored to be a part of your life. Thank you.
One of the things I have been proud of in our relationship
is the honesty we have had with one another. As we have let
each other into our selves, I have been sometimes more honest
with you than me, much to my embarrassment. I have also told
you when I thought you were kidding yourself and tried to point
these things out to you. This was a totally new experience for
me.
Tiffany was an intimate friend with whom I shared much
about you, even from the early days when I lamented the fact you
were married. I feel betrayed by her revelation to these men.
Further, I feel I have betrayed all the trust we built over the past
two years, your trust in me.

It is difficult for me to fully express my love for and admiration of you, when I don't love myself very much. I ask The Boss for help on this so you feel all the wonderful things I truly feel for you, now covered by my shame. Know they are there and feel the warm snugglies, the admiration, the joy of love; these gifts God graciously bestowed on us. Your strength, as fortified, will carry you through.
I love you.
X
P.S. It was Psalm 22. I'm doing the same thing, so I guess it's OK.
X

10/23/94 8:30 PM

Dearest Donna,
        Thank you for your understanding and forgiveness. I know how hurt you were. And I'm glad you are finally seeing an attorney, even if it is only for the restraining order. When you get it, as far as I'm concerned, it is a far more potent legal document than the Order granting divorce. Here, and in most states, orders of divorce are nothing more than legal limited marriages. Divorce is a cutting away. The restraining order cuts his person away better than the divorce. Of course, now it's a matter of property. That Order does not cut him away from your joint property, so he can steal from you legally. Be careful.
Love
X

10/24/94 10 PM

Dearest Donna,
        I can't believe the judge denied the restraining order today after he threatened you last night. This has to be a new judicial distance record for having your head up your ass!
        Talk to your attorney. It's all I know to suggest.
Love,
X

11/3/94 6:30 PM

Dearest Donna,
It was good to hear from you today. I've been worried about you. So, you found out he's hit the till for $5000 in the last couple of months. Don't be surprised if there is more missing. And he threatened to throw away your underwear if you didn't tell him where you hid his guns. How stupid! I'm glad you called the cops and got the guns out of the house.
I'm glad you got out of there too and went down to your Dad's place in Miami. I know it was tough trying to get the kids in all their different schools and going to work and putting up with him while you were there. I'm sorry you had to go back and put up with his verbal abuse, but I'm glad you got a tape of it. Maybe getting residence in another county will help you get a restraining order. I don't know.
I can't begin to tell you how happy I am to be a part of your life again and how happy I am we are talking and sharing again. Nor can I tell you how worried I am about you. I pray a lot for you and the kids. It's just beginning to get nasty. I'm glad I can be here for you.
Love,
X

11/14/94 7 PM

Dearest, Wonderful Donna,
Hooray! You finally got the restraining order! And the darn thing cuts you out of the store at 1 PM. I look forward to seeing you tomorrow afternoon. "Look forward," Hell! I'm jumping up and down with ants under my skin in anticipation of being able to see you in this new state of freedom. Oh, Honey. This is great!
I love you!
X

11/15/94 9:45 PM

Precious Donna,

You are wonderful! Today was wonderful and I was right. I was in awe of your beauty in your nakedness. I still am. I love holding you next to me and showering you with kisses, lingering here and there, as you do the same. Of course, I regret you are not yet fully ready for our ultimate act of love, but I am patient and you are phenomenal.

I love this! I have before planned attacks, yet with you, my plans go out the window and everything seems to flow somewhere beyond where I thought I would be. I also regret your having to leave and not being able to share with you this warmth of love I feel.

It's funny. I don't seem to be able to write poetry. I feel like I'm living it!
I love you so much.
X

11/17/94 11:30 PM

Dearest Loved One, My Beloved,

Tonight was very special for me. Your bath. It was so wonderful to soap your body and wash your hair. We could either look at it as a "Baptism," or a "flea bath." My dear departed Grandmother told me - probably too many times - "When you lie down with dogs, you get up with fleas." Honey, we both agree you have been laying with a spiritual dog, so the flea bath was good.

I felt a bit of resistance from you. Not much. It was as if you were trying to not let yourself fully go into a cleansing mode. Yet even so, I also felt as if the touch of my hand was as soothing lotion for the parched skin of your soul. Where did *that* come from? I'm a poet, but WOW! Oh well. No problem. It will take time for us both. I've never done this before, so maybe it was me. I really look forward to our sacred wedding bath, where we can together wash it all away and join as new clean souls.

I was so sad for you when you told me about letting yourself be picked up and used when you were 15 at the Howard Johnson's bar. Just trying to fit in; be accepted. If I do what others do, then maybe they'll love me too. What got to me is that you said nothing and were motionless throughout. What we do for acceptance! You don't have to be "cold and hard" anymore. You know I accept you, and love you just the way you are.

I love you so much. That sounds yucky. I just don't know any better way of putting it.
Love,
X

11/18/94 11:15 PM

Precious Beloved Donna,

I am so sorry Ralph removed about 25% of your stock from the store. He'll just sell it cheap to buy drugs. Good news about his violation of the restraining order. Maybe he'll be in jail soon.

It was so wonderful being with you today. Helping you with paper work where I could, or just staying out of your way, admiring, and letting you be who you are and do what you do. Then, when all was done that could be done, feeding you and holding you.

Joy came to me as we began to discuss our wedding. I would read from Proverbs 31 and you from Ephesians 5. Oh, my precious one! I cannot imagine greater joy than being married to you. Then, later, as we again lay together in our nakedness, I felt you becoming more free to express yourself as the woman you are. It makes me feel so tingly to ensure this freedom for you. It was funny when you looked at the clock and found two hours had passed while time stood still for us.

I love you with a depth beyond my comprehension.
X

11/19/94 3 PM

Dearest Donna,
It just hit me!! You are an angel!! No wings. No bright lights. Just the ever present glow of your countenance and the music of your heart. Oh, don't worry. You're human too. (Boy are you human!!!) I'm sure you have all the same human failures the rest of us have. Well, some of them anyway. But you are so easy to love and you give love so easily - like an angel.
That makes you a real stinker! You've taken unfair advantage of me. Heck! Phooey! Here I thought you were a people and you're an angel! If you had told me, I might have played my cards differently, but no . . . You lured me in and now I'm hooked. Rnnrow! Rnnrow! Rnnrow! You rascal! You stinker! Dirty trick! Oh well. I'm stuck with an angel now. I guess I'll just have to make the best I can with what you gave me to work with. Nuts!
Love,
X

11/20/94 7:30 PM

Dearest Donna,
Thank you so much for coming to church with me today and bringing the little guys. I'm glad you all enjoyed my friends there and the lunch. I enjoyed watching the guys while you went off and did what you had to do. We had a good time. They wore me out just watching them.
I think my washing your feet, as I did last week, and theirs with yours, blew them away. From what you told me, they have never had personal service from a father figure before. I don't think it had much to do with their being good kids. I think that came from you.
I'm sorry you had to leave with them. Darn it! Well, I'll see you tomorrow.
Love,
X

11/21/94 11:30 PM

Oh Dearest Donna,

I am mixed. You told me today of your conversation with The Boss when you got home after your last visit. He said, "No?" Again? That we would not be husband and wife? He has something better for me? We wept.

I'm sorry you had to hold it in for two days. I'm glad you told me, confronting your fears. Part of me accepts this and a lot of my acceptance comes only from knowing how faithful you are to His words you hear. But know this, if you decide not to follow what he says, I'll fight God for you! I won't win. We both know this. I want you to know I am willing. So I guess we'll continue to grow with one another until He says stop.

I'm glad you finally got permission for us to finally consummate our love. It seems a little late, but I guess the Boss knows what He is doing. As I told you in bed this evening, I hope the Boss is a woman. Maybe She'll change Her mind.

As for my looking like a thirty year old - well allow me to reassure you. You are not robbing the cradle. I'll admit my body hasn't responded like this since I was in my thirties, but you my Precious, are Phenomenal! As we touch, you begin to glow. Your glow quickly becomes softly brighter, and pulsates as you throb with your ecstasy. And the look on your face! It is awesomely beautiful. Your passion takes over, as does mine, and your countenance completely changes.

Your beauty, the beauty of your love in action, is beyond anything I have ever seen. Then, you slowly dim to a moderate brightness, and begin again. Over and over and over, the entire room seems to brighten and dim, brighten and dim, until finally some internal explosion lights you, the room, the sky. The wondrous beauty on your face, about your body is magnificently glorious. This is love I have never before known!

What was really amazing was the little orgasm you had just after I kissed you good night. You turned, bent to pick up your purse and . . . Boom! God! I love you. Don't worry, I'll clean the carpet.

When you called to let me know you arrived home safely, I had mixed feelings when you told me you were walking funny. There was a masculine pride and a bit of regret for possibly hurting you. If you're OK with it, then so am I. I will do my best to keep you walking funny as long as I can.
Love,
X

11/22/94 11 PM

Dearest Donna,

I will enjoy shopping for TG dinner with you tomorrow, as much as I enjoyed being with you this evening. This is so wonderful! It is as if there is no fore play or after play, everything is simply between play. I love you so much. I love letting you be who you are and what you are to me. I love letting you work. I love hugging you from behind while you do dishes. I love it when you hug me while I do dishes. It is as if all the little things make no matter, except the us, and I love the us we are and the us we are becoming.

I secretly hope God lets us continue to grow. I feel this is the way it is supposed to be. If nothing else, we can be an example for others and show them how to achieve this ecstasy. It is too good to keep to ourselves and by sharing it we will increase our own.
I love you, but you already know.
X

11/25/94 11 AM

Dearest Donna,

Damn! You are some fine cook! Wow! All this and she cooks too! I enjoyed so much all of us eating together. It was our first time. God! I feel like such a virgin! Each new experience with you seems to open me further, and I thought I was already open.

I'll see you tonight for the Art Show, dinner and dancing. Another first. I can't wait to see you in your female finery. For me, your beauty is in your eyes and I think you'd look good in a gunny sack. I know you like dressing up and occasionally, so do I. (I really make a Tux look good, but with you on my arm, who would notice me? They would just see the light of my love and pride from being with you.)
Love,
X

2 AM
Dearest Precious Donna,
        I love being worn out by you. You may take it both ways. It was so funny the way the Maitre d' was looking at you so incredulously, not to mention others. When he came out as we were leaving and said, "I know you," after staring at you for an hour, I had to laugh. One of your customers used to seeing you in your scuzzies. I knew better from day one, and delighted in it.
        Then you delighted me again. I hope the photo I took off your face while you were having an orgasm turns out. I don't have the words to describe your awesome beauty in these moments, and I'm glad the flash did not interfere with the following dozen or so. You are phenomenal!
Good night, funny walker.
X

11/27/94 4 PM

Dearest Donna,
        Again it was wonderful having you sit with me in church. I am so proud of you, and I love being with you. I wish you could have stayed, but I know you have things to do. I wish the photo had turned out. It would have been worth a million dollars.
        There is something I don't understand. Were you anyone else but who you are, some of the things you do would drive me up a wall. Perhaps I should put it in the past tense and say,

"would have driven." I'm a long time bachelor. I have certain ways of doing things. Habits. Habits I am comfortable with. At least I was. With you, they have disappeared, fallen away like dead leaves from a tree. I don't miss them. Those things once making up my rigid, anal retentive life style are no longer important.
Love,
X

11/28/94 8 PM

Dearest Donna,
        Well, you've got two violations of the restraining order now. When are they going to put that piece of garbage in jail? I'm sorry you had to close the business today. I know how important it was to you. There is no sense in putting money in the till so he can put it up his nose. It's really no problem. I have enough equity in my home so we can have adequate funds to start over. I can sell it or re-mortgage it or crank it, whatever. I just want you healed from all this. Besides, as I told you before, I think the store is a marital asset and anything you do, he'll get half - or more depending on his lawyer. Hasn't he stolen enough from you? Let it go.
Love,
X

12/3/94 11 PM

Dearest Donna,
        Now it's two violations and three burglaries by "person or persons unknown," and the dog didn't bark. I guess his crack funds are low enough to steal the kid's Christmas money. When are they going to put that piece of garbage in jail?
Love,
X

12/4/94 1:30 PM

Dearest Wonderful Donna,
	Did you know I was burglarized last night? A succuba snuck into my bed about 2 AM and stole the rest of my heart. You stinker! I wish you weren't so tired when I woke up at 6, but I'm glad I let you sleep. You are just so wonderful, and I love you so much.
Love,
X

12/11/94 11:30 PM

Dearest Donna,
	I'm sorry the Boss told you to detach. If it's like what happened after you told me, it's OK with me. Honey I love you so much. It's hard to accept.
Love,
X

12/15/94 2 AM

Dearest Precious Donna,
	I cannot sleep. I am exhausted and elated at the same time. Again, time stood still for us for almost four hours. We keep growing and each of us are letting the things limiting our lives go away. I didn't think anything could be better, yet it keeps getting better. This is only a part of it. It's like the love we share out of bed is manifested in bed.
	As I see more of you, I love more of you and appreciate more of you. I look at where you are in your life and where you have been and what you have tolerated and how strong you are. At least your faith is strong.

Tonight, you brought more joy into my life than anything I have ever known. I have no words to describe my ecstasy, or from what I observed, yours. The second time, you brightened the world as never before. Your explosion was atomic! You said as we lay together, it was the most powerful sexual experience you had ever known. Me too, and I'm so elated for you.

I thought it was just me letting and allowing you, but it is also you, letting and allowing me to be, as we let false inhibitions and reluctances fall away. We are simply on top of the world, and there is a universe in which we may grow. I know we have things yet to share and enjoy. Those cannolis I told you about are at one end. At the other is the mystical merging of souls, rare and fleeting, yet so powerful it makes our orgasms seem like we bumped our funny bones. Perhaps when the divorce is over and things are normal, whatever that is . . .

It is so strange I cannot comprehend how much I love you, yet I seem to love you more, as if we can quantify love. Perhaps it is but a bottomless ocean and I dive deeper and deeper. I don't know. I can only tell you it, and you, are phenomenal.
Love,
X

Noon
Dearest Donna,
I'm glad George hired you, and is giving you part time work. Not only is it something coming in, it allows you the freedom to take care of other things so necessary right now.
Enjoy.
Love,
X

11 PM
Dearest Donna,

You called an hour ago, from dinner with George and the girls. I'm glad you feel accepted there. I must tell you, I have mixed feelings about your cancellation of our plans for tomorrow night. Honey, you deserve to go to the $1000 a plate dinner at Pier 66 tomorrow night with George and the girls. You are a wonderful person and pretty as a speckled pup. I have no doubt you will be the hit of the party, the way you glow with love. I am concerned George "just happened" to have an extra ticket laying around for you. Anyway, enjoy yourself. You deserve it.
Love,
X

12/16/94 3 PM
Dearest Donna,

You called with an emptiness in your voice telling me you were served with the divorce papers today. One would think this is good news, yet I know the shock this brings. The reality is here. In spite of all the work you have done, this is a cold wet towel in the face leaving an emptiness in your gut I heard in your voice. You are vulnerable.

I know you just want to feel pretty and womanly. You are pretty and womanly and vulnerable. Honey, please be careful. I asked if I could be your designated driver should you become a little tipsy, and you said George was picking you up in a limo. I know how this opulence combined with vulnerability can end, and I am concerned. Please be careful.

I love you so much.
Love,
X

12/17/94 - 11 AM

NO!

PLEASE GOD,

NO!

Wonderful sweet denial
  holding back the silent
    scream
of ice picks' agony
        in my ears
vice tight
    on my testicles.
Pain, you ask? No, silly,
  pain is child's play
      this is real!
          and i don't feel a thing.

Thank you blissful denial
  Illusions ripped
      live flaying. How could
          she get so close? How
could I think she...
Oh, it would be so easy
    to label her
        rather than me.
My label is FOOL.

At least
    no longer is
        it sacrilegious
            to ask for better.

12/18/94

Dear Donna,
 It hurts too much to write you, and I still don't feel it all.
It's simply the wall of sandbags I put up to keep from feeling the
pain, started to leak pain through. Soon, the levy will begin to
crumble.
Love,
X

EPHEMERAL EPIPHANY

I wait for her call
  telling me how much
    she hated it
        because she loves me
driving me away.
                *

"Everybody gets
the woman they love...
        but me."
Thank God!
Sorrow and self pity
  together at last.
    with sobs and tears.
May they all come
  leave none behind
    I miss her too much.
                *

"I'll give it six weeks..."
  and lose
    another six weeks
      of my life
          for naught.
                *

Beethoven's Ninth
* cranked full bore*
*   to drown the screams*
after the son-in-common law
* asked for my help...*
*   with her.*
*

You take my vulnerability
walking in dry dusty fields
drink my water
quickly abandon me
for another.
You leave me lost, crying
no sense of direction
as mealtime
and storms approach.

*

Friends flock
* bringing love's shelter.*

*

I rejoiced in
* giving you all*
sharing you with my friends
*   the world*
lifting you up
* washing,*
*   anointing your feet*
*   your soul*
sacred service to you.
Your cruelty is kindness.
*

I freely ran to the mirage
  swam in wondrous sand
    blinding my eyes
      with the phenomenon
        that is you.

                    *

Now,
   the pain.
Let it flow!
   cleansing my soul.
I rejoice in pain
        as I rejoiced in you.
You may keep what I gave,
   as I will cherish
        the ecstatic mystery
           you gave me,
   for I loved giving it
      as I will again
          but...
                    not to you.
                  *

Your cruelty is kindness.

12/20/94

Dear Donna,

       Damn, it hurt! Yet, I keep throwing sandbags in the breech, watching them wash away. I try to hold on to what you said, about God having someone else in mind for me, yet it slips away and I am swept downstream in the torrents of pain. Then, I grab for a straw and swing to the bank; I climb, momentarily, only to slide back in to the maelstrom. At least it eases for a while.
Love,
X

HUMAN EXPERIENCE

For years I climbed
        love's
    loose rocky mountain
      gently inserting
  pitons of vulnerability
     tieing strong braided rope
         of purpose
     balanced in ecstatic awe
       upon its top
deeply inhaled
       fresh sweet joy
wondrously amazed
      without understanding
         its grandeur
entranced.

Pushed off,
    I tumbled
  over sharp rocks
       and cliffs
     down the talus
        smashing
  tearing
     parts of my body
       soul
into pain's deep valley
     avoiding oblivion's
        flash flood.

I expressfully experienced
   all this
     and lived to climb
      larger, stronger mountains.

I extend my human range
    farther to go.

123

12/21/94

Dearest Donna,

I cannot tell you how incomprehensible and painful your betrayal of me is. I cannot tell you because I do not know! Just as I could not comprehend how much I love you - it is the same. I loved and trusted you completely and fully. The joy and ecstasy I felt from and with you was also beyond me.

Funny. The greater mass of people struggle just to be happy. A chosen few know joy. I felt alone in my ecstasy with you, high enough to make Everest look like an ant hill. It is not a small fall.

I must tell you the ecstasy was worth this pain - and it is not over! I gave you everything, including my inner child, and now it feels like you are stomping on him as one would wipe shit from the bottom of their shoe. Loving you fully, accepting all of you, knowing your weaknesses, led me to heights I did not dream existed. The pain deepens and I can look for depth of the same order.

It is strange to feel this hurt by you and still love you so much? I shall love you from behind my cloak of pain and not let you in again. You have also lost something by this betrayal. Everything about you I accepted, as you did me. Until this. This is totally unacceptable, your behavior is unacceptable. You told me so many wonderful things, like this was the first time you were ever totally accepted. It's gone now. So is the wondrous sexual love making. I had to specify. For a month it seemed with every breath I took, I was making love with you.

I hope you find someone with whom you are as acceptable and compatible. Someone with whom you can enjoy both your deep and shallow orgasms as we did. I don't think you will, but I hope so. I hope you can trust them and be as free with them as you were with me, but I don't think so. I hope you can have hours of pleasure with them as you did with me, but I don't think so. I think this is something you gave up for the new store, so maybe it wasn't as important to you as it was to me. I have filled ashtrays and cried a lot, but not enough. I must go to bed. It's 4 AM
Love, X

LOVE IS NOT ENOUGH

in sleep
i roam, flail the bed
searching
unbelieving aloneness.
waking
emptiness and loss
fills, aches my body to tears.

lifted to heights never before;
abyss dropped unstopping,
plummeting so far
through sharpened nothingness
into nothingness,
the dim point of light
above me
is the raging   pits of hell.

merciful bottom arise
through the nothing
terminating velocity.

i reap what i sow
then love is pain
and lovers are masochists
in disguise.

be pain the price of ecstasy
then pay the demanded dues
but know... and risk again
or die.

she too weeps
but not alone.
her sorrow offset
by goal realization.

justification fails
facts remain.

i shall canine share my death-walk
where greater fidelity
is purchased
at a smaller price.

i dress in clothes of sorts
and the bed is made in preparation
for another day, yet...
all things are not in order.

how dare you! tell me
my pain will deepen
my human experience!
your justification fails,
as did mine!

let resentment reign,
for a while; then return, oh denial
provide ease to this interminable being
as needed or 4xd. wait, oh pain,
on more auspicious times.

i gave blood today...
it was the last thing i had to give.
totally empty.

let gratitude begin... the phoney kind
cling to anything until you know
even though
you cannot comprehend lost value.
amen.

had we loved each other more,
i would have exploded.

2/25/94 7:30 AM

Dearest Wonderful Donna,

Finally, some acceptance and gratitude have caught up with me. I wanted to share with you my limited understanding of our place in each other's lives. First, know I will always love you and be grateful for your presence in my life, but it shifted last night with a sweet ker-thump.

In grieving my loss of you, I felt like I was grieving every loss I ever had, for you completely touched me everywhere. It was very painful and cleansing. I feel both emptied and filled. What a wonderful gift you gave me. As tears fill my eyes now, they are tears of joy and gratitude, with only a tiny bit of sorrow mixed in.

I have shared my grief with a number of my friends - with whom I felt safe- and amazingly found out who understood and who didn't. Many were angry with you because of my pain. They could go no further and simply figured you were wrong. I feel sorry for them. I know how much you love me, and how much it hurt you to free me. You are truly a good and faithful servant to God and may he bless you and protect you always.

I am glad you stayed the extra four days beyond when you were told to leave. (Remember how Abraham dallied when told to sacrifice Jacob? He took three days to go a half-day's journey.) It tells me how much you loved me, and allowed our last time together to be my gift to you. This is something you deserve in your life on a regular basis. Besides, it deepened my love for you and made your loss more painful. I needed the extra scouring powder for my soul cleansing. I told you before ;pain is mandatory. Suffering is optional. By fully feeling our pain, we avoid the suffering.

You are very wise in many ways. Perhaps you know exactly the nature of the wonderful gifts you gave me. They are still joyfully jumbled within me. One is awareness I am leader of the pack, and with you, I belonged in a different pack on this earth. You knew a year ago, but had to show me. Thank you for your time and love.

I was talking with Anne last night. She told me, "You had to have the hot fudge sundae to get ready for the banana split." Anne is a minister in the Church of Universal Life, New Age, hates "religion." You are fundamental Christian, and both of you say the same thing. I think it is funny, and now understand what both of you say. Sort of a different pair of socks to be knocked off. She also said, "Be careful of George." Like you, she knows things. Even though it is different, I still love you very much, and do not want to see you hurt. You've had enough. It is also soon time for you. Speaking of George, I called in my suspicion, to see when he purchased the "tickets" for the $1000 a plate dinner. The party was free, and open to the public. Be careful.

I went to an AA meeting last night. For the first week of your loss, I was so screwed up I forgot about the Serenity Prayer. I finally remembered about it and for two more days could not put the word "Serenity" in the first line. I knew "Give me the grace to accept, . . . " was wrong, but simply could not figure out the word serenity belonged in the Serenity Prayer. Yesterday morning, I looked it up. It helped. That's why I went to a meeting. I was so screwed up I could not remember basic tools. And yes, the thought of drinking myself into oblivion crossed my mind. I'm an alcoholic. I'm supposed to have those thoughts. I just don't have to act on them.

At the meeting, we have five minutes of silent meditation to begin the meeting, during which I learned how out of balance I was. I laughed at myself. There are many ways of describing this imbalance, but the Hindu Chakra system is common among my friends. My Root Chakra (sex and anger) was swollen, huge, as was the heart Chakra and the Chakra of courage. The crown Chakra was large but discolored - it is supposed to be violet - and the third eye of insight and Chakra of intellect were tiny. The throat Chakra was perfect blue, as I express myself well. What was immediately funny to me was before you in my life, the root Chakra (sex) was always so small. I had to work to envision it large enough to be in balance with the others. Now, I'm going to have to work to shrink it to its proper size to be in balance.

Another tool of acceptance in the program is, "Everything is as it is supposed to be." You call it the pan theory; everything pans out for the best. Also, two rules: One, don't sweat the small stuff. Two, everything is small stuff. This does not minimize your magnificence or importance in my life, only my ego driven thinking of the way I (a large capital I) think (thought) it was supposed to be.

Well, my precious one, my life today is still bitter-sweet, but far more sweet than bitter for you being a part of it. Know this. You are Woman! A wonderful, fantastic, phenomenal Woman. If you can't believe it, then believe I know it. You are an angel too. Your gift to me of sharing your power in such a beautiful way I shall always cherish, as will my awakening to the mystery of love. These are gifts few have the capacity to either give or receive. Thank you from the deepest nooks and crannies of my soul, for you reached me everywhere.
Love,
X

12/29/94

Dearest Donna,

What the hell happened? This reality Sucks!! I would rather live in my possibly neurotic illusion of ecstasy than accept your betrayal. You are the easiest woman to love I ever met. You give to all equally of your friendliness and gentleness. Your sex appeal is backed by enormous sexual power. I've watched it for over two years now. One of your most attractive features is your loyalty to your marriage vows, even married to an unfaithful druggie. Or, was it because his parents were rich?.

I loved you totally and fully, allowing you to be who you are, and God help me, I still do. In loving you, you became as my flesh and were comfortable with me, and I you, as never before. When you left, it ripped away my flesh. I can't sleep. I close my eyes and see you and George in bed, knowing the ecstasy we shared, the love we shared is not there. Within forty eight hours of the most powerful sexual experience of your life - with me! - you are in bed with George. Two months ago you said you didn't even like him. Is this so he will set you up in business? I know George professionally. He seems like a nice guy. (Why do I want to kill him?) He's just another guy with a lot of money. God, Woman! You have other options! Are you just an emotional/financial butterfly? (To keep a butterfly you must kill it and pin it to the wall.)   Is this about your financial responsibility the kids?

You took off the red coral ring I gave you. The promise ring. Last year, when you took off your wedding rings, all I could do was kiss your bare breasts and hold you next to me in our half nakedness. Where did this new found sexual freedom come from? Don't we mean anything to you? I saw you walk into the Courthouse today. With George. Sorry I spied. I had to see the two of you together when you didn't think I was around. You were holding hands as we did and he was wearing the same shit-eating grin I wore. It could have been me. Hell! It was me twenty three days ago!

My consolation in all this is maybe I really fucked you up. You now know what it is to be totally loved and accepted and the accompanying ecstasy. Really loved. What happened? Did it frighten you? I'll grant you it is scary, but this? There were so many things about you I loved. Your fidelity. I thought you would make a great partner were, as the doomsayers predict, we all catastrophically forced into a survival mode. Now I see if the next campfire were larger and more meat hung on the tree, you would go. Why is it easier for me to think less of you now than to accept I was right in my former evaluation of your fidelity?

Of course there is more! You loved me and I had no money. It was just me. That is so precious to me. It set me free to do more efficient things. Our love removed my limitations. I had always been concerned had I money, it would be the attractor not me and I know I'm too dumb to tell the difference. Maybe I'm still too dumb to tell the difference, so why bother staying poor?

Your error is not only in your pattern, but in expectations of fulfillment from your pattern. Why do I bother? You told me a couple of days ago I had to forgive my parents. You told me God told you to tell me this. You know, I was taught by Mother when you love someone, you have an obligation to them, no matter how abusive they are. Mother was abusive. Mother always threatened to abandon me. Yet, I loved her. This is the way I grew up. Find someone who threatens to abandon me, then let them abuse me and I'll stay so I won't be abandoned. Until the abuse becomes too painful. Then I run. In later years, I disliked her behavior. I felt an obligation of care for her. I filled my obligation and left the instant she became abusive (30 seconds to five minutes,) reversing the abandonment role. As painful as this is, I want to stay with you. In spite of this abuse, I'm not ready to run from you.

We are all the product of our parents, to some degree and in some way. Perhaps many, like me, live in some of their neuroses. Patterns of life, once established, are hard to break. They are only broken when the person in the pattern realizes how self destructive, or self limiting, it is and becomes tired of destroying themselves and those around them. You have not come to this realization, yet, and it works for you. As long as it does, there is no hope for an us. Hope is frustrating and futile. Maybe it's my pattern, and it's not working for me.

Sam bought me a copy of *The Velveteen Rabbit*, by Margery Williams, for Christmas. I want to read you something from it.

"When a child loves you for a long, long time, not just to play with, but REALLY loves you, then you become Real. ... When you are Real you don't mind being hurt. ' ... "It doesn't happen all at once," said the Skin Horse. "You become. It takes a long time. That's why it doesn't often happen to people who break easily, or have sharp edges, or who have to be carefully kept. Generally, by the time you are Real, most of your hair has been loved off, and your eyes drop out and you get loose in the joints and very shabby. But these things don't matter at all, because once you are Real you can't be ugly, except to people who don't understand. ... The Boy's uncle made me Real."

We were both loved by one another. We were both becoming real. Which of us is more comfortable as a toy? Do we want to become real humans? You use "God" to justify your behavior? Can you justify this? Did God tell you to do this as He told you we would not be husband and wife? I hope someday you really want to be Real. I know you still love me and still desire me. Part of me finds this very flattering. Today, I want you back, but will you stay? Tomorrow, I may not. Someday, when you just want to be loved as you once told me, . . . who knows? I justified my behavior - sexual abstinence until the restraining order, and the emotional involvement during abstinence - with love? I justified poverty to wait upon what you said. But, you were still married. My justification led me to many sorrows and some growth from it.

Do you feel an obligation to continue the phone leash because you love me? Or for future wealth? The most important thing you ever said to me was, "I don't care how much money you have, I love you." I believed you then. I believe you now. I also believe you lack the capacity, faith and belief to act on it for any length of time, unless the money is there.

Maybe I didn't love you after all. Perhaps I "financially fail" and self impose poverty to be abused and abandoned to fulfill my illusion of love? Or am I afraid I will not be loved for who I am behind money and will make a mistake? (Mother was afraid Dad's ex-wife under California law would take 1/2 of every thing they ever built, so they built little.) Did my loving you and you loving me in this new way, significantly change my illusion of love? I don't know, now.

I don't know the answers to any of the questions I've asked you in this letter. I don't know if I'm asking you or asking me. The next time I see you, I'll ask. Maybe I will hear the answers you give, maybe I won't. It all depends on what I want to hear, to ease whatever pain I'm in at the time. We'll see.
X

FAMILIAR BEHAVIOR

She let me in
          to see
     that which no other
had ever seen before,
          as she saw me.

Getting past the used part,
     she was
          a beautiful phenomenon.

I went forward,
          fell on my face,
While she
          retreated in fear,
               diverting to the security
                    of familiar behavior;
          tolerating, believing, justifying
                    anything, ...for the security
                         of familiar behavior.

When she busies her self
     no more,
          with dots and dittles,
               and reflects;

Her loss is not me,
          but what she was becoming
                    with me.
I grieve it sorely,
          not only for her,
                    and my ego, but...
For all man.

We explored and nourished
each other
into the frightening depths of
Our souls
growing in and with.

We validated, worked,
and shared
our awesome ecstasy
until...
I required security
of familiar behavior.
The loss,
grief
behavior
Are Mine.

January 3, 1995

Dearest Donna,

It wasn't time for you to go, it was time for me to look at me. You had to go so I would look. You left in the only possible way you could. I am so sorry you had to do what you did. It was my pattern, not yours. I can only imagine how you must feel, and your hurt from this is the only thing I regret in our relationship.

I also feel badly about my bitterness toward you in the early part of my question letter. However, I needed to see it was my need for security - not yours - and my pattern - not yours - driving me - not you. As it stands now, my bitterness is really at my own pattern. I know you are wise enough to understand this, and know you, and your love, made me face it with enough emotional impact to have it sink in.

Of all the gifts you gave me, the most precious one is me. It took the precious gift of you to do it. I do miss you, and the growth I enjoyed with you. I only hope my gift to you is as important and cherished as I cherish yours. To say "thank you" seems so trite and inadequate.

Know this: I love, honor, respect and admire you totally in your fullness as a woman. (I also know you are human.) Also know I would have been (and were it the case, still would be) proud and honored to have you on my arm as my wife. You deserve no less from any man. You may borrow these as your boundaries if you like. The loss I grieve most is what I was becoming with you. God hasn't finished with me yet. This is simply another starting place.
Love,
X

SOLACE

I sit near Mother Ocean
Her chill wind of reality
   caressing my face.

Gentle waves shore lap
and fragrant sea-oats
   dance lightly in the breeze.

Solitary gulls surface skim
seeking nourishment
   as I seek solace.

My calm comes,
as hers is, knowing
   all is right, feel at ease

1/3/95

Dearest Donna,

Time to revisit my question letter of the 29th, and see what perceptions have changed. First, we were both loving and got better at it. For the most part, I imposed my parentally installed fear of financial security on you. Where ever I talked about you going for money, it was me being afraid of it. Weird! Fear of financial security?

Yes, you cut my heart out. It gave me the emotional pain to cut away these issues. We both enjoy sex, especially with each other because it was different from anything we had ever known before. This is why your act is so incomprehensible.

I've known about this threat of abandonment thing for a long time. I use to accept as a part of me, as well as the fear of financial security. No More! You showed me my love is pretty powerful stuff. I just don't fully know how, yet. Your removal of my ring was simply adding to the betrayal. Did this trigger other betrayals? Am I still on your hook?

It's true. You know what it is like to be loved by another human. You already know what it is like to be loved by God, and obviously, you love him better. I do see a hint of dual loyalties in you, with two, or more men in your life. What are my dual loyalties? If I seem bitter, or like I don't trust you, remember, grief breeds doubt.

I justify my behavior with my narcissistic mother's fears. And therein is my dual loyalty! I am loyal to Mother's fears as she instilled them in me, and to you! Right now, it feels like I'm wearing boots a size too small on a 50-mile march. It will get better. The pain I now feel is nowhere nearly reflected in the statements. I justified a lot to maintain my denial of the pain I now feel.

It is quite possible you are a gift, sent to prepare me. If I can get through all this BS and figure things out, **then act on them**, I'll be in much better shape to enter a real relationship. No, not right. We had a real relationship. One of the things I really liked about us is the ease with which "stuff" fell away from me. I changed willingly and joyfully, and it was an improvement! Love removes limitations. So, I guess it's time to ask some more questions.

Was I addicted and this is withdrawal, or am I simply a romantic fool? Neither. Just a normally screwed up human being. Hey! I got an answer! You told me a year ago (1/3/94), "God said no to us." Threat of abandonment! I took this bait like a hungry snook at high tide after a finger mullet! It was the form of control and conditional love imposed on me since the beginning! Your love seemed unconditional, yet I guess we all place conditions on our love. You gave it freely and equally to all, up to a point . . . but these are my questions.

I have never before tried to analyze a relationship. Why now? You are very important to me. We were very important to me. Things are as they are. Perhaps then I can see what I did "right," as well as "miss the mark." Then, have confidence to know these things, rather than throw bath water, baby (you) and all away. Everything I did in our relationship was geared toward building an us, . . . or was it? At least, I have no doubt, if I made a "mistake," I picked the right person to make it with!

I lowered my boundaries for you.   A big boundary: I fell in love with a married woman. I have an aching and overwhelming need for the security of home and wife. Yet, note how I talked about **your** security! Your financial security can be replaced with my emotional security. Is that right? I was extremely secure in your love, until you betrayed me. I guess it is if "emotional security" is the same as the security I found in being loved by you and in loving you.

Since you betrayed me, how did I betray you? By lowering my boundaries, I deprived you of my full self. I also deprived both of us of the ephemeral sense of oneness, a rich gift of intimate relationships. The situation I created by crossing this boundary is mutually exclusive to oneness. I set a poor example by essentially stating, "It's OK to lower your boundaries to fill your needs." Honey, I guess I grieve the loss of my old pattern wherein I was "comfortable" with the pain I created by lowering my boundaries.

I also did not provide you with a clear definition by example between "silly rules," boundaries, and walls. There may be other ways also, including using you to fill my needs?

However, this "need" is normal in most and part of it is normal in me. Mine happens to be "excessively normal." (I love my euphemisms.) Then again, so is the power of the love I have to offer you to meet these needs.

     It's getting better!

Love,
X

METAMORPHOSIS

The joy of youth turns
  to bile of betrayal.
The inviting pond
  over which he swung
    and gleefully plunged
Turned
  to strong acid
    searing flesh and sinew
  away, exposing
    raw and bleeding soul
bandaged by anger
  wrapped over tears.

My error brings
  no comfort,
    solace.

O Sweet Death
  come
    be my bride!
Share with me
  your infinite joy
    as I would share with her.

Let this end come quickly
  if at all.
Prepare me for another life
  a life beyond…

1/6/95 7 PM

Dearest Donna,

You sleep now. Your call to me at 3 . . . I could hear the exhaustion in your voice. It seems you busy yourself into oblivion as I once drank myself there. At the time I thought it was better than feeling the pain.

I'm really pissed at George! This is no business deal, lest he deals with monkeys! I see him taking advantage of a vulnerable, screwed-up woman who would rather be taken advantage of, to keep busy than face the pain. As painful as it is, it is nowhere near as bad as the clusterfuck you are working toward. You and the business, for you ARE the business, deserve more respect than he shows. I know. Feed the kids. It's a good excuse. Not good enough!

Another thing, you created a monster in me. I see more clearly who and what I am. I wish you could see who and what you are as clearly as I see you, or at least as clearly as I see me. I was not aware of my power until you, ... and you still are not aware of yours. Force is concentrated power, and you apparently spill and waste your God given power. I am saddened by this.

This monster you have created. Anyway . . . "best friend" is reserved for the woman who is to be my wife. You then, are - or will be - a "close intimate friend." There was a time when I equated the threat of abandonment with "love." You must have loved me; you threatened to abandon me three times and finally did. Oh, I know you are still there, and in spite of my definition, you love me in a way I have never been loved before. And I love you as well, in a way I have never before loved. You abandoned me as your lover and future husband.

The problem is, I still love you as much as I always did and in the same way. I learned from you abuse is not love. I deserve more. I no longer see the threat of abandonment as a "garden wall" in which I may be abused. Where I was before, I was second fiddle to Ralph. Fine. You were married to him. I provided you with love, friendship, emotional support and validation while I patiently waited for you, and YOU WERE WORTH IT! and still are! You provided me with the most magnificent and glorious experience of my life! Schiller's Ode to Joy doesn't touch it, even as set to music by Beethoven.

Like you said, "Don't go backwards. Go forward, or sit down." Honey, I can't go back. I will not go back. I will not return to the role of providing you with support, in second chair, while you spend time in another self-destructive relationship. Not again. At least before, I had hope of being your husband some day. Although fading, it still burns within me. With you, or without you, I will go forward. No doubt, in unfamiliar territory, I will trip and fall on my face. I just did with you, but I fell forward! For me to sit in second chair now, is too painful. For you to ask me to put my life on hold while I watch you destroy yourself is a form of abuse. I reject it! I find new tears to cry each time we speak and new pain I thought long gone. God told you to leave, yet we stay, and staying brings only more anguish.

Being close to you with hope is wonderful. Being close to you without hope is self-flagellation, and I don't do that any more! I deserve the whole magilla, the whole nine yards. I've tasted it. I know what it is like. I won't settle for less. In time when my healing is done, if you are still there, I can be your "close intimate friend." Now, our bond and my memories of the wonderful love we shared are too strong, too painful.

If you will not come with me, I will go on alone, healing from the wound your absence creates in my life. There are many kind and loving men out there. Men who will see you as did I, love you as did I, honor and respect you as did I and as I still do. If you will not come with me on the rest of my journey through life, my prayer is you become clear enough to find one of them. You are a magnificent phenomenon, and deserve no less. Were George to put a fence of respect between you and his blindfold of lust as I did, he would see it too. Please hold yourself open to one of them and closed to those who don't deserve you. Otherwise, you cast your pearls before swine.

I love you and the word love has a new and glorious meaning for me, a sacred mystery you, and only you ever introduced into my life. If, as you say, there is to be another for me, then how can I see her when I am so blinded by my love for you? If, as you say, there is to be another for me, then I admire you and will always honor this sacrifice you made for me. I would only ask you honor it and respect yourself as I respect you.

May God reward you and bless you in ways you never thought possible, as He has me.

One last thing. I imposed my fears on you. I imposed my fears on you in a tone of voice I have never used with you before, yet one that reminded you of the one your parents used when you pulled this same stunt in your youth. What I am trying to do here is validate our mutual power. I had the power to impose my fear; you had the power to change the tone of my voice. This power we have cares not how we use it. I have seen my fear and my pattern, as you have seen this loaded gun within you. This new awareness for both of us shows our growth.

Since I can no longer support you in any of the ways I once could, let me suggest you lean on Dave for business advice. Then, get "married" to Misters Smith and Wesson, until the right man for you appears. That kind of bigamy is O.K. Please be proud of me, for this is my first excruciating step on my new path. I would prefer walking on hot coals.
Love,
X

1/8/95

Dear Donna,

I've gone over a lot of the questions I asked with you. Time for, hopefully, a last go round. Your response was, you were angry with me for imposing my fear of abandonment on you regarding your vulnerability. O.K. Let's look. You were served that day with divorce papers, "had" to leave me, and allowed yourself to be used for four minutes to "prove me right." It seems my tone of voice, one I had never used before, reminded you of the shaming your family put on you. Funny how our power doesn't care what we project. I projected my fear on you; you heard old tapes and responded with old behavior, projecting your requirement for tone on me. I'm so proud of you for ignoring the old stimulus in a recent family meeting! I guess the garden I gave you to grow in worked. Your grew. Our forgiveness is mutual.

I see now my error is in my pattern, and my expectations of fulfillment from my pattern. I do not have an expectation of abandonment, I am attracted to the threat of abandonment. If I am a good boy, you won't abandon me. I sobbed for three hours yesterday and cried out, "Why did you hurt me. I was a good boy." Then it hit me: I put me in a prison where I can be a good boy so someone can abuse me. Betrayal is the ultimate form of abuse. This abuse is self inflicted with the collapse of boundaries. I misinterpreted it as the ultimate from of love. I live in the prison's fear of economic security. If the pain is too great, I run to another prison.

One thing bothered me; your comment about being a "classic under-achiever." I have achieved great things for which others were rewarded because I did not feel myself worthy. Hell! 'I've been doing so much with so little for so long, I can practically do anything with nothing.' Time for a change there too.

I did little in this relationship to be a "good boy" so I would not be abandoned. Although, this is how I was taught to build a relationship. I lowered my boundaries to do it. I was building an us compatible with my fears.

I like being a "good boy." I like cooking for someone who needs and appreciates my food, my nourishment. I like being a good sex partner with someone who wants to be a good sex partner with me. I enjoy loving! I will enjoy it more when I can do it freely without the threat of abandonment, and the accompanying abuse, as a part of the package. I would still do it all over again. With or without this stuff. . . .

By the end of the evening, I was so screwed up I wrote in my journal:

I do not know whether I loved or performed as a good boy so I could be abused. I don't know if I gave love or not. I do know abuse is not love. Whatever love is, can I receive it? Can I give it? I only know I'm physically cold and confused."

What a life! I guess I had better go somewhere else for an answer.

Love,

X

Voices
*   human voices*
strong acid in my ears
*   dripping on my soul*
my hackles up
as they rip me apart.
Voices
*   like vultures*
*   circling*
*   flesh picking*
saying "I love you"
*   as the key*
hiding motives
*   to claim more of my soul.*
Voices
*   claiming authority*
*   to know what's best*
*   to take me from me*
in my vulnerability.
Voices
*   inside, say*
Trust your body
Listen to your hair
Look at your wound
Stay away... safe!

Nobody's home
Nothing's left.

1/8/95

Dear God,

I've got a feeling if I write to you, I'll get an answer. I'm confused. I don't know if I loved Donna, or if I was a "good boy" so I could be abused. I can't trust my "friends." They want me to throw it all away and start over. I can't trust her, she'll just hurt me again. I can't trust me. I'm too confused. You know more than I do, so I'll tell you what I think I know and You give me the answers.

You know how I was raised. My garden wall was the threat of abandonment. If I was a good boy, I wouldn't be abandoned. Being a good boy meant taking abuse, thinking it was love. Mom told me in many different stories - catching the iron about to fall on my head, pushing me under the bed during the air raid, not having her placenta squeezed during her appendectomy - of "saving" me because she loved me. When she first told me, I didn't know what a placenta was! Now I wonder if it was so, in her narcissism, she could keep her whipping boy?

I didn't think much about Dad's sexual molestation of me. I was accustomed to abuse and thought it was love. I could intellectually stuff it. But 12 years later, when Zeke the bartender told me he used to serve Dad at Virginia's Place (the local whore house), it was a betrayal of our "intimacy." I could no longer intellectually stuff my pain and in five minutes, started drinking. (This betrayal of my sacred intimacy with Donna was even more painful.) Bottom line, I confuse abuse with love. So, the question is do I love or am I a good boy so I can be abused? I don't know.

My illusion of myself is I am a kind, loving person. I have done that. But Why? So I can be abused? This permeates every aspect of my life: professionally, socially and personally. As long as I keep putting out, "Abuse is love. Love me. Love me," that is what I'm going to get back.

Now I see everybody as takers and abusers, if not in fact, then potentially. Even the T.V. (notice it is on mute.) They want to take my money and offer very little in return. Like the "guaranteed bug killer" I bought out of the comic book - 2 - 4" 2x4's with a sign on one saying, "Put bug in circle and smash with other block." It was OK. It worked. My friends want to take my time to abuse me under the guise of love. I can't really see too straight. I have produced and done well in most of my jobs. I've screwed the pooch a few times and been shat upon for it.

I'm more sensitive to abuse now, but I just run away when it gets too painful. I'm tired of drawing it into my life! So, your mission , if you elect to take it, is to help me quit drawing this into my life and let me know if what I do is really love or performance.
Thank you,
X

1/9/95

Dearest Donna,

I was really screwed up a couple of days ago! The only person on the face of this earth I trusted was me. My inner voice was telling me I was screwed up and I could easily believe it! I didn't know if I loved you or if I was just setting myself up to be abused. Anyway, I wrote a letter to God and this morning I got an answer. I was led past *The Song of Solomon*, Fromm and Buscalia to *The Prophet,* giving me this answer to the question I asked:

. . . Speak to us of love . . .
When love beckons to you , follow him,
Though his ways are hard and steep.
And when his wings enfold you, yield to him,
Though the sword hidden among his pinions may wound you
And when he speaks to you believe in him,
Though his voice may shatter your dreams
 as the north wind lays waste the garden.
For even as love crowns you so shall he crucify you.
Even as he is for your growth so is he for your pruning.
Even as he ascends to your height and caresses your tenderest branches that quiver in the sun
So shall he descend to your roots and shake them in their clinging to the earth.

Like sheaves of corn he gathers you unto himself
He threshes you to make you naked.
He sifts you to free you from your husks.
He grinds you to whiteness.
He kneads you until you are pliant;
And then he assigns you to his sacred fire, that you may become sacred bread for God's sacred feast.

All these things shall love do unto you that you may know the secrets of your heart, and in that knowledge become a fragment of Life's heart.

But if in your fear you would seek only love's peace and love's pleasure,

Then it is better for you that you cover your nakedness and pass out of loves threshing floor,

Into the seasonless world where you shall laugh, but not all your laughter, and weep but not all your tears.

Love gives naught but itself and takes naught but from itself.

Love possesses not nor would it be possessed;
For love is sufficient unto love.

When you love you should not say, "God is in my heart," but rather, "I am in the heart of God."

And think not you can direct the course of love, for love, if it finds you worthy, directs your course.

Love has no other desire but to fulfil itself.

But if you love and must needs have desires, let these be your desires:

To know the pain of too much tenderness.
To be wounded by your own understanding of love;
And to bleed willingly and joyfully.

To wake at dawn with a winged heart and give thanks for another day of loving;

To rest at the noon hour and meditate love's ecstasy;
To return home at eventide with gratitude;
And then to sleep with a prayer for the beloved in your heart and a song of praise upon your lips.

Kahlil Gibran

If this be love then, for the first time, I have loved, and loved well. I have been wounded by the sword and been shaken to my roots and seen the foul earth to which they cling. I removed the husks covering the sweet corn of my being, standing naked in myself, and am being ground to whiteness for the potter's fire. I have known the pain of too much tenderness and have felt the cold north wind lay waste my garden. I have found the secrets of my heart to become a fragment of Life's heart.

I have accepted abuse for love instead of accepting me. I have sought those who would abuse and betray me, believing it to be love, as my parents taught me. I have been a "good boy" in my fear of abandonment, rather than for its own sake, yet this time I loved you simply for the joy (and pain) of loving and being loved. I have yet to cry all my tears becoming an empty vessel to fill again and in this same way for even greater joy.

In spirit, this love was doomed, for I crossed a sacred boundary and was removed from this Garden of Eden, as brusquely and as painfully as were our common ancestors from theirs. Yet the lessons of this experience, painful as they may be, shall serve me.
Love,
X

1/10/95 8 PM

Dear God,
I kind of like writing letters to you. I have another request. I think Donna thinks I'm about the best thing to come into her life, as she was in mine. I know she loves me. I know I love her. So do you. She gave me up on your orders, showing how much she loves both of us. You also know how anal retentive I am. If you can't get us back together, please bring a man to her, worthy of her, as you have made me. Reward her every way you can, short of taking her to Your bosom. She is to me a very special person on this, Your earth. I sincerely pray for all good things to come to her, and I hope I'm one of them . . .
(*no . . . **no** . . . no . . . **No, Dummy! NO!** ...... wait.*)

OK, Boss. I'm not sorry for asking. I guess you do have something better in mind. Thank you so much for putting her in my life as your gift to me.
Love,
X

1/12/95
To Donna's Children:

Dear Kids,
KNOW THIS: I know your mother better than any man on this earth, including her father. I tell you she is the most wonderful, loving, phenomenal woman I have ever had the joy of knowing and loving. My deep sorrow now comes from the realization and acceptance we will not live together as husband and wife, and I cannot be a stepfather to and for you.

Also know your mother told me three times these were words she heard from God: first over a year ago; second in November, the day after we were discussing our dreams for our wedding, and finally in early December. She loved me in spite of this. With all the things happening at the house to distract her, I felt more love from her than I have ever felt before in my life. Loving usually takes some work, yet with your Mom, it was the easiest thing I have ever done. We were together because of our deep love for one another. There was a lot of pressure on her: from me, from God, from everybody.

This love is still there for both of us, but has changed (I think) because of our trust in God. I can no longer love her as a wife-to-be, but more so as one of my Dearest friends. Forgive me; it will take me time to make this transition.

They say, "Boys marry their mothers." (Actually, women who remind them of their mothers.) Then boys, if you do any thing less, you will make a great mistake. I know what to really look for in a woman because of her, and because of her, I now know how to really love a woman. I plan to do no less, and I hope you do even better.

Girls, my wish for you is you each find a man who loves, honors, validates and respects you as I did your mother. I have never known a greater love in my life. Yes, there was great pain associated with this great love, because for an instant, while she was under all this pressure, I doubted my trust in her. I used this pain as both weed killer and fertilizer, to kill fear weeds within me and to grow open eyes to see things I never saw before.

You may ask, "If they love each other so much, then why don't they get married?" I don't know. It sounds good to me. It could be God has plans for all of us are much better than anything we could ever dream of, as I dreamed of your mother as my wife. I do know this: your mother was and is a precious gift in my life I will always cherish. You may also like to know, YOU all are gifts in her life, she too cherishes. (That is what she told me!) She is human and will make "mistakes." Please forgive her as I have. Treat her as a gift in your life, not as a toy to be played with, but as a gift to be honored, trusted, cherished and respected. She deserves it, as you deserve to give it to her.

Love and best wishes for you all,

X

1/15/95 10 AM

Dearest Precious Donna,
Your coming over tonight for our healing excites me. I slept little, 1:30 to 2:30 and 5 to 7:30. I'll try for a nap this afternoon.

There are some things I need to clarify. Most important, I knew all along you are a human being. You are no more or less a "divinity to be worshiped" than I am. We are divine only in that we, like every one else on this planet, are children of God. I held the nature of our relationship sacred and honored its sanctity. It was the first time in my life I have ever done this, and maybe I wasn't too good at it. On the other hand, it is probably the first time in your life any one has ever honored their relationship with you in this way. If so, I can understand your confusion and fear I was beginning to worship you instead of God. This is only a part of the reason I was so deeply hurt.

I look back now, laughing at myself for words I wrote to you and about you I did not understand at the time. I no longer apologize for the ones about you. You are the mirror of my soul. As Milton said in *Paradise Lost*, "What thou seest, what there thou seest, fair creature, is thyself." I only saw myself, good and bad through you.

I also laugh at what I told you in the car that afternoon about how you couldn't help it. It was your tremendous sexual power coming out "sideways." Please forgive my rank stupidity. I KNOW how well you control your sexual power. It is not the issue. Perhaps with all that was going on: me, God, you, George, kids, divorce, harassment, and so on, and the gun installed by your parents, you couldn't help it. I was right and I was wrong. Yet, we are both amazing! First, at how four minutes in your life could so dramatically impact mine, and second for how both you and I have used this impact to grow. One thing for sure, we are both "tough acts to follow."

In one letter I wrote, "Grieving your loss is like grieving every loss I ever had, for you touched me everywhere." I did not understand at the time. Later I ask, "Did this betrayal trigger old betrayals?" I did not know then the answer was "yes!" I never fully felt the pain of my father's "betrayal" and have carried it with me all these years. Your four-minute betrayal ripped the scab from that festering wound, allowing it to heal. So my precious one, you were not responsible for all the pain I felt; you are responsible for allowing me to feel and deal with it. In my letter to the children I put "mistakes" in quote marks. I am here to confirm what you already know, God makes no mistakes. We do.

I wrote at the end of a letter to me I have not cried all my tears. I do miss you, and the joy and the ecstasy we shared. I will for a while and that is OK. It was the most magnificent experience of my life. I would be foolish to dishonor it. Another lesson is the magnitude of our joy and ecstasy is directly proportional to the magnitude of our love for each other, not just mine or just yours, but ours. I now pity those who struggle to seek "happiness."

As I begin to unwrap myself from my own self centeredness, I also begin to see what this did for you. I am proud of you. I am proud of me for my contribution to you. I am sure I only see part of it now, and maybe more later. I see my validation and my acceptance of you, confirming that validation, made you stronger. I love the way you recently confronted your mother's shaming and George's discounting you for making him late for the "early bird special."

Although I don't see it yet, I hope you become truly aware of the magnificent, special and powerful woman you really are.   (I hope I become aware of the magnificent, special and powerful man I am.) I don't see it because I'm not around you much anymore and you were just beginning to grasp it when we parted.

One thing in your growth brings mixed emotions to me. You tell me for the last month you have not required the "one or two beers to calm you down" in the evening. Also, you are cutting back on your meds. This is the time I have been out of your life, and tells me two things: 1. Your growth is as phenomenal as you are. 2. My continued presence in your life as your lover was beginning to do more harm than good, dividing you when you need to come together. A part of loving you is wanting those things for you in your best interest. Right now, I as your lover, am not one of those things.

Mixed emotions: It is as if a big, blurry 90% of me wants you back in my life, growing as we were. The smaller 10% is sharper and stronger. Mixed emotions.

Anyway, my Precious, I thank you for your gifts to me, and I thank God for his gift to me in you.
Love,
X

1/16/95 4 PM

Dear Donna,

First, let me thank you for last night. I am glad you let me show love for you in many of the same ways I did before. I am pleased you took some of the grilled chicken salad with you. It was pretty good and I'm glad you enjoyed it. I also enjoyed washing your feet, and your washing mine, and "anointing " them with the lotion. Then, holding you as we wept together. Thank you also for delivering the letters to the kids.

By allowing me this demonstration - within the limits of your comfortability - it made me feel as I have truly forgiven you. This morning, it seemed like the pain left - some sadness remains, but the pain is gone. I now feel like I can really sleep!

Yes, some resentment remains. It, like leaves on the hedge I pruned to near nakedness while I pruned away my old fears, will fall away in due course. As you put it, "Life is not instant mashed potatoes."

We have both grown in our togetherness and in our separateness. I am still uncomfortable in my "new suit." It's like the coat collar is turned under and I can't get the fly up. Oh well. I'll grow into it. "It's not instant mashed potatoes." I think I'll work on the fly first. It's a guy thing, you know.

Thank you.

Love,
X

Lost
   in familiar places
   where all is, races, but...
   doesn't quite register...
yet.

Lost
   in my reclining chair
   TV, ice tea are there, but...
   isn't quite ...
strange.

Lost
   between my ears
   after one thousand tears, but...
   before my heartache...
empty.

Lost
   chores half done
   stop, then one
   where did it go?...
the day.

Lost
   This new robe I wear
   old things I foreswear
   nothing's the same...
ever.

3/2/95 5:30 am

Dearest Donna,

Last Sunday, when I confronted you with the accusations about George, you said, "Why don't you ask me instead of having these conversations with yourself?" I would love to, but you're not here. I have no one else to talk with! Were you here, you could not be there, so it would not even come up.

You said "get analytical," so I did. Anyway, I have finally become analytically resentful. You say you still love me, want me, etc., etc. I hear you. I see you too. Love is action. Love is sharing. Love is being with. Love is growing with. I have no doubt I was loved by you, so I know what it's like and this ain't it!

God told you to get out and you did. O.K. You love God. That is fine. You love God, you don't love me, so stop saying it. It sounds like that old left-handed love I have seen others use to justify their errant behavior. "I loved him so I killed him." Donna, I loved you. You know what it is to be loved. Look at us, and tell me you love me. You may "have feelings" but, this is not love. Not of me, anyway. Of God, yes. You can tell me God loves me for getting you out of the way, but you can not say you love me. Unless it's like one of your customers in the shop. This kind of love you can save for someone who appreciates it. I don't. It doesn't get any more personal than this, so I am taking it personally.

Be happy. Your mission - to get out of the way - is accomplished. I no longer doubt God and if he has someone else for me, those old feelings for you will no longer interfere. However, since it's only people who are telling me this . . . well, I can doubt them.

I still have mixed emotions about you. Thanks to you, I know what I have to offer a woman. I'm sorry it will not be you. I hope for both of us we can again know the joy and ecstasy we once shared with each other, and never again feel this pain.

If you really love me, pray that I can stay cold towards you. It ain't easy. By the way, I can say I love you with a clear conscience. I have been there for you -save once. I have respected you, your feelings, your life. I have honored you and us, been proud of you, validated you, accepted you, opened you, grown with you and never stopped loving you with word and deed, even when the deed was simply waiting. I have sexually pleasured you (and you me) beyond our wildest dreams and shared this joy and ecstasy with you. I have felt the pain of too much love, and used it to grow, setting aside antique fears, as have you. The love you once had for me, and I you, with it's power did these things, and I am eternally grateful for them.

Gratitude, like love is also an action. My action is to remove myself from your life as you have from mine. Staying is suffering. The pain was mandatory; the suffering optional, not one I choose. Will I ever see you again? Probably. Hopefully long after my firing mechanism is completely disarmed. Stay well.

Love,

X

HEDGE

The buds of my naked
hedge turn to small
leaves, yet stems remain.

I see growth, and naked-
ness, sometimes focused
on leaves, othertimes stem.

The cup may be half full
but, it is filling. Where did
she go? She who stripped me?

I forgive, am grateful for
the denuding. I resent
her absence in my healing.

3/5/95 6:30 am

Dearest Donna,
        The potatoes are cooked, this batch anyway. There are so many things about us I do not understand. I, the great intellect, am at a complete loss.
        When I began to love you, my goal for you was your freedom from the clusterfuck you were in. Of course, I told you my "ulterior motive" was you would be free to choose me. Almost worked. I saw you put down so much, you could not thrive and reach your potential to live and enjoy life. I wanted you to be free to do these things. I also wanted to provide an environment for you (with me) where you could grow like God's favorite flower.
        So what happened? It was me who got the freedom. It was me who was putting me down all these years. It was me who had not reached my potential to live and enjoy life. I had been in a prison of my own making. Self-institutionalized. Through you, I have been pardoned and today your divorce is final.
        I can identify with long term cons hearing the doors clang behind them as they step out of the joint onto the street. I know why so many of them return. It's scary as hell out here! I guess that's why I hung onto my desire for you these past couple of months. I was afraid to let go. I'm still afraid, but I'm letting go.
        Has this changed my opinion that you are the most wonderful, fantastic, phenomenal woman I ever met? Not at all. Do I still think you would make a wonderful wife for me? Absolutely! The problem is you have your freedom to choose and you didn't choose me. Unless it's me, who you choose is none of my business. Your reasoning for this choice is the only thing I do understand, and is one of the many parts of you I respect.
        I thank you for being in my life and God for putting you there. (I still hope She will change her mind, but it's OK if He doesn't.) From somewhere it seems like I was given the courage, or strength or faith to accept you are not now an integral part of my life and I can go on without you as a partner. Old Cliff and I

are going to become good buddies here, 'cause right now life
seems like another cliffhanger and God is all I have to hang onto.
On the other hand, I lacked imagination to envision anything or
anybody as wonderful as you in my life. What's next?
Love,
X

KEEPSAKE BOX

*lovingly, gently
i lift her out
of my heart and soul
setting her in
memories' treasure chest*

*carefully wrapping
in clear glass
this precious treasure
protecting her with
newspaper
peanuts and prayers*

*a joyful heart
closes the lid
sealing her off
until . . .*

3/7/95

Dear Donna,

I want to talk about George. It's funny. At first, I thought he was taking advantage of your vulnerability and wanted to kill him. It was despicable! (Fifteen years ago, I might have done the same thing in his shoes.) Now, I have good news and bad news. The good news is if ordained, you and George will be lovers: perhaps sooner, perhaps later. The bad news is it may kill him.

In my jealousy, I asked you if you were. You response, "Not yet." You will be. I know you better than anybody, including your parents. I can pretty much predict your behavior, sometimes better than my own - except for that night. I knew you were going to stay with Ralph two years ago; I didn't want to believe it. I knew it wouldn't work. I knew what was going to happen after the party, but I didn't want to believe that either. If things keep going as they are, you two will be lovers.

Right now, he is hooked . Frankly, I don't care that much about George. This is for you, and me, so I'll continue. First let me validate you by saying George's financial investment is safe. His emotional investment may not be. I hope it is. He is a nice guy and you deserve one. I just don't know if you know how to treat one, as we expect.

He has a lot of advantages to offer you that I did not. He is younger and financially successful. (You admire his business skills.) I have a lot of advantages he does not. I have far more depth than George and am able to express it. He spent his time, perhaps more wisely than I, making money. I spent the last ten to fifteen years differently.

We have a lot in common: both members of our respective churches for the last fifteen or so years, both took you to them, both divorced, both finding you one of the most loving women we ever met, both very much in love with you and both desirous of the unconditional love you project. It is something few men are privileged to even see, much less find themselves in its aura. One fatal flaw we have (in your eyes) is we are both a "little" anal retentive. This also means organized and task disciplined. From what you tell me about him, I see we both

carry it over into our personal lives. Our homes are both neat
and squared away. (With four kids, forget it! Is he ready?)

You told us both you are not for sale. His money turned
you off. Unfortunately, you are lying. You are for sale and the
price is our heart. All of it. More of it than we think we have,
and believe me: with you, it's there. George is coming off a sand
lot, headed for the emotional NFL, with all its bruises and pain
and perhaps a Super Bowl Ring at the end.

You are a meal for an emotional gourmet'. George is
used to emotional fast food - perhaps like me, some even made
from road kill. If he eats this meal too quickly, he will get one
helluva stomach ache, perhaps fatal. I hope he enjoys and
appreciates the presentation. He should delicately taste and savor
each morsel you offer and approach you as though he were
eating Basmati rice one grain at a time. Should he be fortunate
enough to have the entree ordained, you are a meal fit for an
Emperor.

Gourmet meals are expensive. The price for this one is
time and willingness. Willingness to have his false identity
stripped away; sometimes given joyfully, sometimes ripped
painfully. This is the price of love. Can he afford it? Is he
strong enough? If, however he feels completed within himself
already, he should go back to McDonald's, or he will surely die.
The journey is fraught with pitfalls of his own making, the ones
he has tried to so carefully cover, as have we all. These pitfalls
are where he has hidden his pain, the pain already within him.
You will not cause it. You will expose it, allow him to feel it and
rid himself of it. Years ago in a similar situation I wrote:

> *Standing at the gates of hell,*
> * gently ringing Satan's bell*
> *Waiting, waiting to be let in.*
> *For here's the journey's start,*
> * not for the faint of heart*
> *And not to enter is the greater sin.*

Later, confronting Satan in the same poem, I wrote:

> *He shrank back aghast,*
> *   then uncovered my past*
> *And I stared down a cruel, evil chasm.*
> *Past the pits of hell,*
> *   where not even a knell*
> *Could be heard. My guts started to spasm.*

So, I have seen the place where I was and now am in familiar
territory: Hell! Even then, I knew I would have to return
someday and closed the poem with this:

> *I wave good-bye to hell,*
> *   with it's foul and evil smell*
> *Returning for another larger load.*
> *For the work has just begun,*
> *   we have Old Scratch on the run*
> *As we trudge down Destiny's road.*

I have the experience. (Prophetic, wasn't it?) It is a
frightening journey. What he enters into here is no game for
children; it is a dangerous hunt for men, and its reward may not
be what he expects. We seek the prey and find the prey is us.
I'm telling you this, because from what you say, George is going
in unarmed. Further, I say with all humility, you are a stronger
woman for having known me. A lot of the "normal B.S." that
may work with others, will not work with you. Unfortunately for
me, the strength I gave you, you used to increase you resolve on
following the "yes"/"no" directions you receive. Continuing my
dream of walking through life with you as my partner is simply
beating my head against a wall. (It's such a lovely wall!)

 If he takes this journey, he will need others for support as
I did. Those who are perhaps on the fringe of his acquaintances.
Those whom he has observed to be silent in their discussion of
others, silent out of respect rather than fear; those who
understand the truly mystical quality of life rather than
intellectualize it. My Pastor was one. Others he will find in
those who have surpassed their suffering. (He should stay away

from shrinks and counselors. Generally, they use their profession
to cover their own pitfalls. They will label him with some God-
awful disease instead of recognizing his humanity, prescribe
expensive medicines and not give him the opportunity for
growth: only the opportunity to pay them.)

I had a circle of friends for support. Half of them I cut
away with a curt phone call, for I knew they lacked the capacity
to support my growth. They would bring me back to where they
were comfortable with me. I found others who understood; who
had gone beyond the rigid intellectual thinking that permeates
our lives today.

As he grows, he will increase his ability to give you his
heart. When you are certain of it, if ordained, you will be lovers.
In the meantime, he will accept your diversions from him, as I
did. He will "understand" your emotional upheaval with the
divorce, your loss of me, your distractions with the house, the
kids and on and on and on. He will patiently wait, as did I, for
you to return fully the fullest love he is able to give you. When
you give it to him in those moments, it will be ecstasy he never
knew before. Yet, he will wonder and rationalize why you
always seems diverted off on some tangent instead of fully
returning the love he gives you? It must be ordained!

I've been married twice, had more than my share of
"girlfriends," quick contacts, etc. Until you, I never before truly
loved, or made love with a woman. Most of my adult life, I
studied and practiced sexual techniques so I would know how to
please a woman. It almost seems like a waste of time. Putting
the cart before the horse. The ecstasy I knew with you, and you
with me, was simply because we deeply loved one another at that
time. The source of my ecstasy was in the complete giving of
myself to to the sacred us - not you, but us. That is the lesson I
validated with you.

Why didn't it last? You say, "God said no. There is
someone else for you." It was not ordained. A cynic would say
you trophy hunt for nice guys with whom you can find a fatal
flaw - our anal retentiveness. I know out of my own fear I sought
women I knew were unavailable. Then when it was over, I could
say, "pheweww." Like attracts like. Maybe you do the same
thing in a slightly different way. But, I fooled you! I lost some

of my anal, some of my fears. Some were easy, others
excruciatingly painful, yet what you offered made them seem
valueless. Either way, God or cynic, you were right.

You hooked George this past Christmas as you hooked
me the Christmas before. I backed off out of respect for your
choice to make you marriage work. I knew it wouldn't, but it was
your choice. When it didn't, I came in like a mullet-chasing,
hungry tarpon on a moonlit night. George doesn't have to back
off. There is no marriage in the way for him to respect. It would
be best for him if he did. You do have more than your share of
emotional upheaval for him to respect, yet you are strong.
However if he doesn't, you will go elsewhere. You know what
you deserve.

I hope he lets you decide when you would like him to
take you and the kids to dinner or a movie. You will need time
to heal and for him to grow. I hope he focuses on the business
and his growth. His financial reward is far more certain than the
expected ROI on his emotional investment! It won't be easy.
Particularly since you are in business and he sees you daily. I
know how desirable you are. I know what it is like to want to
swallow you, devour you. God! It's powerful! The unavailable
is the most desirable. It was much easier for me. I just got out of
your life for six or seven months. Even dated someone else. He
can't fully extract himself because of the business.

You still love me, in your way, from behind your wall. It
helps provide you with a diversion from George while you heal.
We still desire one another, but you will not act on it. You desire
is not ordained. Were it ordained, this letter would never be
written for George would not exist in our lives. Understand, if
you had wished to cross the boundary of non-ordination, I would
have done battle with God Almighty to protect and preserve our
growing relationship. I valued it that highly. No mortal man
would have stood in the way. With me, there will be no "us" for
you, nor George. You deserve better. Also, when I see you now
and observe you physiological response to my presence, it still
gives me false hope. I deserve better and obviously need time to
get past this false hope - for my healing to complete.

I don't know how much you have told George about your
past, but your choice of George and me shows your taste in men

is improving. Our choice of you shows our taste in women is improving. George's hope lies not only in his growth, but also in what he can offer you for your growth. Hopefully, besides the store.

I hope it works for you guys. He is going to have to make some big changes in his ability to accept you just as you are. When he does, he will see how phenomenal you really are. You are going to have to make some lifestyle changes too. I will vouch for your willingness to do so under the right circumstances. None of us have the capacity to change who we are, only in who we think we are. You were worth the lifestyle changes I made. If you really want him, you will come around a little too. I caught you (you caught me?) in a real mess. Maybe after you heal . . . I don't know. That is why I say it might kill him.

Yes, I still love you in spite of it all. Part of loving you is wanting your joy, your happiness and well being. Your highest good. How this is done is your decision, not mine. I thought I could provide it. Whoever does can't have a third party (me) in the way. You will use me as another diversion from the us with him. You already have plenty of diversions. (I have never seen anybody take so long to get a phone installed!) I would only get you back if God tells you "yes." He's already told you "no" with me. Our great love was not enough and it's a little late now. God knows what He is doing. This is who you are. I must accept it.

Whether it really works or not, when he thinks he has you, he will be the happiest man on this planet. He will be for as long as he is with you. Should it end with him as it did with me, without emotional preparation, he may kill himself, for you will be the greatest loss he will ever know! Hell! He's not even there yet, and already he got drunk and arrested. Should he ever pull a more serious self-destructive stunt, it might hurt you.

I've had the last ten or fifteen years for healing and introspection and getting to know more about myself, and others. He's been busy making money. It will not protect him from you as it has protected him in the past. Nor will all his intellectual knowledge. You have far more depth and insight than he currently has the ability to realize; it's well hidden under your

lack of "formal education." With all my self knowledge, you
exposed in me festering pain of which I was completely unaware.
You knew. Your loss almost killed me.

I hope he honors you. Respects you. Accepts you.
Validates you. Appreciates you. You are worthy of it. I hope he
honors and values that which is between you; your relationship.
Because of me, you know what this is. You deserves no less.
Love,
X

BONJOUR, RENE'

That I think matters not at all.
It is but moss upon the wall
of who I really am. The rock
and mortar of my soul does lock
my essence and is the power
guiding my life hour by hour
through deep valley and mountain top
until I finally scrape and stop
trying to paint the moss with thought
washing away each new should, ought
and chip away old mortar past
set each rock in new mortar last-
ing. Life changes, begins again
moss seals mortar, now becomes when.

3/13/95

Dear Donna,

I deleted yesterdays letter from my computer as surely
as I deleted my impression of it. New awakening. I kept trying
to put you in a box. A large box but no less a box. George's box
is smaller. Most of us guys do this in our relationships with
women. You fit no man's box! My honoring you and accepting
you - even when it drove me nuts - let you know I was increasing
the size of the box I was trying to put you in. Oh, for sure, you
had stuck yourself in a box and you didn't like it. (You still have
some boxes and triggers left. We all do.) I couldn't exactly see
it. My validation of you let you know you didn't have to be there
any more.

As now, when I don't really like it, I have honored and
respected your closeness with Dad. (See what you've got me
doing?) Being without you is like having freshly amputated
arms and legs, yet watching new ones grow in their place,
wondering what I am going to do with these "strangers."

Another aspect of your love I really accepted without
realizing your intensity, is *matros,* motherly love. I saw the
agape, Dad's unconditional love; *philos*, our brotherly love,
laughter and closeness; and of course *eros* in our overwhelming
sexual desire for each other. You are also trying to fill the role of
patros, fatherly love, in providing for the children and that is
what this is all about.

A lot of guys see women as packaged sperm dumps and
in recognition, these women then see us as penises with wallets
attached. Your expected behavior is based on how much money
we flash and spend (on you). When all else fails, we say, "I love
you," then expect you to come rushing into our arms and live
happily ever after, or at least until the next morning. Thank you,
to the best of my knowledge I have never been one of these.

You are not one of these either and this is just one of the
many reasons I fell in love with you. It is only a small subsidiary
of your closeness with Dad. The problem you must recognize is
most men have no concept of *agape*, even an intellectual one;
and many of those who do, like me, believed it was for
everybody else, not us. From you, it is more deadly than the

sweet allure of your pheromones. We intuitively desire it
because we know we should have had it a long time ago. What
we got was put into boxes, where we learned to put others into
boxes.

When I saw it, recognized it in you, I was overwhelmed.
I knew what it was, I had just never seen it before. Why do you
think people came into your store? Why do you think some were
uncomfortable? Not knowing what it is, many of us just try and
stuff it in our little boxes of experiential dealings with women. "I
pay, you give." You are easily misinterpreted! Remember, **who
you are** fits in no man's box or illusion of who you are. We are
misled by your signals. (I wasn't. I knew the difference.) I was
so overwhelmed by the "big three," *(agape, philos* and *eros)* I
honored, but did not focus on *matros*. Although I was aware of
your efforts at *patros*, I felt a little patronizing toward them.

I knew, and was confident in this knowledge, I could
provide for you and your children, if by nothing more than
through marketing you in your own store. (You are so easy to
market and it would have been a joy!) I knew that I could
finance it through the sale or mortgaging of the house. I know
the estate is going to pay off big time, and people would much
rather read about a happy ending in the way they are used to than
in the way this book ends. BUT, I wanted to wait. Not to see
what you were going to do, but wait until you heal more and
could devote more of yourself to the business. You <u>**are**</u> the
business and when you are "not all there," not settled in and fully
comfortable within yourself, well, . . . I did not think it would be
a good investment. (My "thinking" is sometimes the wrong tool.)
The investment is in **you**, not the walls and stock. Look at where
you are. Running off after George - or his patrotic carrot, taking
care of his problems, still trying to shape up the house, going "90
to nothin'," and the phone is turned off in the store. Not a good
sign after two months. Of course, I have not checked new
listings, yet.

The flip side is I would have been in a subordinate role.
I would have been where I always was, making a lot of money
for others. Perhaps you knew better than I, I really belonged
elsewhere.

I have no idea how to keep you out of the clusterfucks you keep getting into - my perception. I am still jealous of the bond you are establishing with George. "If you hang around the barber shop long enough, you get your hair cut." A lot of guys can handle boundaries, if you establish them further away. Unfortunately for you, this is another function of *patros* which you have not demonstrated to me, except in the store where you have a "professional" boundary in place.

Putting on 10 or 15 pounds won't do it. Most guys don't realize the source of your beauty and attractiveness is in your eyes. Most guys won't see that, or the 10 or 15 pounds. We see the love in your eyes, without really knowing what it is and think it is for us as we have been conditioned to receive it. You know our "little heads" do most of our thinking in intimate relationships. (What a waste!) We get too close and we get blinded! Then, blind-sided. Anyway, Honey, I think showing your *agape* from a greater distance will improve your chances of having it understood and respected, as well as satisfying your attempt at *patros*, if this is what you want.

I told you before, in a matriarchal culture, you would be elevated to the status of "Sacred Queen." I have already. You are. You deserve to be. But the reality of the patriarchal society in which we live will allow only those of us who understand these things to see you this way. Plus, we have to give you your humanity too. This is a tall order. Thank you for recognizing my ability to temporarily fill it, and protect you from those who don't. Were it I could continue in this role. It is one for which I was designed.

Always remember what Dad told you about taking care of you. I know it is tough. "When you are up to your ass in alligators, it's hard to remember your objective was to drain the swamp." From my ego centered perspective, I would hope you honor our past relationship by settling only for what you deserve; to be honored as the very human, Sacred Queen you are. This is the biggest box I have to put you in for shipping away.
Love,
X

CLASSICALLY TRITE

The Siren's song from ecstasy's flowered field
I heard, seeing not the jagged rock or bones
Or foul rotting flesh of others, I did yield
And plunged into, ignoring sharpened stones.

Swept and battered on the empty promise reef
I lay awash in blood stained pools of sorrow
'Till I took the rode of life within my teeth
And pulled to safety, healing for the 'morrow.

With freshed waxed ears as Ulysses crew, I left
Her isle and upon it my own demoned fears
For those who also would sail her way bereft
Of sense, with longing too find themselves in tears.

Let winds of life blow my ship to distant shore
With these lessons behind. Penelope there
Waits her husband, and I have adventures more
Challenging my soul for a good life to share.

3/15/95

Dearest Donna,

The Ides of March. The day Julius Caesar was assassinated. I have just returned from delivering the last letter to you and wanted to reflect on and repeat what we talked about. The last shall be first.

Your validation. I have been so wrapped up in my stuff, I have forgotten to validate you, as I did earlier. I wanted to let you know what a good job you are doing in helping me make my emotional U-Turn. Part of my anal retentiveness is in my emotional inertia. This morning you physically faced me to the west wall and said, "Look. Your focus is on me, over here." Turning me to the east wall, "Focus on Dad, over here." It helped. We both know how thick I am.

You are a gift! I was thinking about a baseball cap my parents bought me when I was eight or nine years old. It was bright blue with a fore and aft lightening bolt on it. I called it "Flash." I loved that cap. I got into a couple of serious fights over it - as serious as a nine year old can be - when other kids would snatch it off my head. I wore it to rags. It's gone now, only this memory I share with you.

I haven't changed much. You were a gift from Dad to me. I would have fought Him to keep you proudly "on my head." The real gift was in your opening of me like an old, tightly sealed can of sweet, yellow cling peaches. Right now, I am just looking at the glistening surface, barely touching and tasting the nectar. If I eat of me too quickly, I will surely get a stomach ache. Others have seen this but, unable to open the can. You did. Or at least provide the powerful experience of love to let me do it, or Dad do it. I don't know. I do know it took what it took to get me here, where ever this is.

It's like I was so used to jumping from box to box on internal or external command, as I had seen others do or allow themselves to be done unto, and now find myself in a boxless box. I must explore it carefully. I am used to defining myself by my limitations, my boxes.

A week or so ago you shared with me about the spontaneous orgasms you had, like the one when I walked into

the old store. It happened a couple of years ago. Boy, did that
ever push my ego button! I guess when I told you a few months
later I could give you an orgasm without taking your clothes off,
you were laughing at me twice. First, because you already had
one, and secondly, because I didn't know; it, like our love, was a
gift from Dad. It was no different than finding myself with an
erection simply by thinking about my incomprehensible love for
you: a powerfully normal physiological response to the power of
our love, as your fat lips are to your desire. Strange for me how I
can also get this response with lust, but then I'm focused on lust,
not love. Lust doesn't seem as powerful.

I remember thinking it was about the time I knew I did
not understand or comprehend how much I loved you. It was the
most powerful thing I ever felt in my life! And there you went
and "popped off" one. It was the power of my love, our love, not
my handsome face. There was no doubt we desired to
consummate this powerful love, but this just validates what I
learned when we did. It was our love that made our "love
making" so ecstatic. It had little or nothing to do with all the
"sex manuals" I had studied and practiced.

This knowing is something I deeply wanted to share with
others in our life - obviously by lifetime demonstration. A gift to
my fellow man. When we put our love, acceptance, validation,
respect, honor of one another, ourselves and the bond this creates
between us as Dad's children first, the enormous sexual
experience is simply His gift that follows.

I was sickened by my former stupidity in this. I have
forgiven myself. I didn't know any better. I am still sickened by
what I see in others ignoring this wonderful gift. Using the boxes
of our own making in which we place ourselves and others.
"You fit in my box, Dammit, or I'll beat you to death!" Well, . . .
it is scary to let go of our boxes, either our own or the ones in
which we try and put others, or even the new ones we have
jumped into. On the other hand, I have now experienced a taste
of this great reward. Other rewards will follow, as long as I keep
on doing what I'm doing: tightly clenching Dad's anchor rode and
pulling myself along it.

You, my precious gift, unlike Flashes' wearing to rags, are also strengthened. For me, this is the toughest box to get out of. We embodied everything I grew to believe about the most intimate form of man-woman relationship. I don't know if I am again limiting Dad's power to bring one "more suitable" into my life or in my childish petulance, thumbing my nose at Him. Probably a little of both. (You must have been talking with Him. You don't use words like "more suitable.") This new relationship has its growing pains too, and I guess I'm entering the "terrible twos." Don't worry. I'll grow out of them. I'm too scared not to.

Today, this Ides of March, the expectation of permanence with you, my Caesar, was assassinated. I know deep within me, I did everything I could to the best of my ability as a human being to make us work. I had "reasonable" expectations of permanence, even after Dad said "No." You were still here, then. That was your humanity, not Dad's will. I simply chose the right person to grow with temporarily, not permanently. You, like Flash, must go into the box of precious memories. When I am more grown than now, perhaps a "teenager," I can lift you out as I once lifted you up. With more gratitude than I, the poet, can express, I am,
X

3/18/95

Dearest Donna,

I was triply hurt by our phone call yesterday. Good news: my spontaneity is improving. I began to feel it almost as soon as we hung up. I called with good news; I found an expectation to let go of. I was happy and free. Then, you told me about George spending the night in bed with you - "fully clothed." Clothed or not, it makes no difference. I thought it cruel and did not expect it. Next to you in bed is MY PLACE! Although fading, I still feel that way in my heart and soul and I'm doing the best I can to let go of it. That's one. I shared this brand new - I mean brand new infant, a few hours old - awareness with you and you smothered it as an overwhelmed mother would smother her own new born. That's two.

The most devastating part of this is I know you also have these lingering feelings that next to you in bed is MY PLACE. Oh, I know you don't want to "go there," any more than you were going there the day you had the spontaneous orgasm. Nevertheless, your fat lips tell me they are there. I'm not yet as ready or eager to meet your new lover as you say you are to meet mine. At this point, I would rather validate your awareness of George's screw-ups than his progress. I also understand and appreciate your human need for intimate companionship.

How would George feel if he knew I was suckling your breasts last week while he was avoiding arrest out of town? If he knew we still had a level of intimacy he may or may not have yet reached? How do you think I feel knowing - from you - your level of intimacy with George is increasing? Doesn't this conflict with your prediction that Dad would have someone in my life before yours? Please give me more time to heal! Please give me time to establish a closer relationship with Dad! I know these things intellectually. I'm still thick and it takes time for the rawness of this deep wound to heal so I may absorb it emotionally.

No, you are not responsible for my feelings. YOU ARE RESPONSIBLE FOR YOUR BEHAVIOR. I assume you did not tell George about my suckling your breasts. Why? Because it would hurt his feelings? Because it might impact your business relationship?   Who you tell about what you do is also your behavior. You are going to do what you're going to do, just don't tell me for a while. From what you told me about George, in the past he regarded you as a sweet piece of tail he was trying to buy. From the first day I saw you I regarded you as a wife. Initially and admiringly as Ralph's, because of you, not him; later, hopefully as mine. Thanks to me, George is either growing or searching for different tactics.

I know this is a problem for you because we have spoken intimately, openly and honestly since day one. It is a hard habit to break. Perhaps you are trying to gently let me in after the fact? Either way, I'm not ready.

There is more good news. In church today the sermon was about temptation and idolatry; the reading was 1 Cor.10: 1-13. It finally hit me about my idolatry. When Jacob wrestled with the angel, he did not know who he was dealing with. I valued us so highly and was so afraid of losing our relationship, I would have stepped up and punched God in the nose. Back to the abandonment issue.

Donna, God blessed me with my children, some good friends and always takes care of me one way or another, in spite of myself. Never before has he blessed me with anyone as precious as you and I was afraid. You were - in your former capacity - such a precious gift. The most powerful event in my life! I simply need more time to see you in a different box - a different type of relationship, (without my desire) and to establish my new relationship with Dad.

Beyond idolatry, at a more earthly level, I also see a failure in me to demonstrate my ability to fulfill reasonable expectations of *patros*; i.e. support the kids. George has and can. This, of course, sets up conflict in me with what you told me in the past. Your behavior, of letting George sleep in your bed, (increasing intimacy) can easily be interpreted, or misinterpreted, as a reward for his ability to apparently satisfy this driving need of yours. This pushes my shame button. I know my current skills. I know I could have easily accomplished this in my "normal," left-handed way. With the power of our love behind it, duck soup and no sweat. (I sometimes wonder if you two aren't playing a mutual con game? Each pretending to *almost* satisfy the other's needs until one of you has their goals met.)

I guess it also seems to me like you were discounting the power of our love. I knew it didn't come from me, only through me. It was really His. Seems like God is turning his back on me, after showing you to me. Your beauty. Your love. Or is He leading me into another store to shop? Or just teasing? I still don't understand. I know things are going to work out for me, one way or another. I still have a hard time seeing God as an Indian giver. I don't know. Look at Job. I guess he thought he had everything too, and wound up so much better off than when he started. I obviously do not possess Job's kind of faith, yet. Should I share good news with you in the future, please don't do this again. I'm tired. You really don't have to point out my lack of faith this way.

My idolatry really hit home as I worked on this. Funny.
As you read this, you can see. I couldn't see it even though I was
saying it. If I loaned, or gave, my son a precious gift and he was
going to punch me in the nose rather than return it, well, . . . I
would not give my "blessing" to him either. I really don't know
how to accept His gifts. It's now easy for me to see my "sins" are
based in fear; this one based in the fear of abandonment. So,
what I thought I let go of yesterday was a fear of "non-
permanence," abandonment, rather than the "expectation of
permanence." It is euphemistic and silly to let go of "reasonable
expectations," when I can let go of negative fears. The prodigal
returns.

Lastly, let me say I can easily believe you slept
untouched as you said. I can also believe that won't last for long.
You are human, remember? The night you came over and snuck
into my bed, the following morning, well prepared, I did not.
Even sleeping, the power of your love is great. Or was it my
love for you? Our hormones need attention, yet what you offer is
a new and different kind of satisfaction. Your telling me of your
growing intimacy with George still hurts. Please don't tell me
about it for a while. Anyway, when I hear about things
prematurely, as you can see, it screws-up my head. Be gentle.
Although "pain means I'm in error," I'm human too.
Love,
X

NOISES

Door noises
imagining
presence . . .

feeling it not
nor
will I . . .

ever.

3/21/95

Dear X,

Ding! Ding! Ding! Dingbat! Boy are you dumb! She never admitted to betraying your love or trust. She never asked for forgiveness for betraying your love or trust. She asked forgiveness for **HER** behavior. She never asked forgiveness for how her behavior impacted you! She had the balls to tell you it would be "a growing experience." Well Hell, Baby! Look at where you've grown to! To a point where you can see this whole thing was about **HER** and you only played a "supporting role."

Look at the reality. Where is she now? With George. Excuse me? This is love? I don't think so! You know what love is. You know what you gave her. You know what it did for her. Hey, did you have a spontaneous orgasm when SHE walked in the room? I hope she has good luck with her next one!

And the voices in her head she calls "god" to justify her sociopathic, sweet cruelty. Do you really want anything to do with that? Does she "*...do justly, and love mercy and walk humbly with thy God?*" You didn't. Thank your own God for getting you out! She loves without risk because she can turn it off any time it gets too close. Is love without risk love at all? You were close enough to see her wounds and didn't put it together. You offered her the ambrosia of love. She tasted it and fearfully rejected it. She did not want to remove her limitations. Her choice and she made it.

All right, Dumbshit. If there is a next time, don't get so wrapped up in "us" that you forget about you. Pick one who is really available to accept this ambrosia. You've got eyes. Quit accepting and "understanding" screwed up behavior. Accept and understand that it **IS** screwed up and you don't have the power to change it or make it any better. Make sure your wants and needs are satisfied as you satisfy the wants and needs of your partner. If they are beyond her, tough shit. Find another! Forget about abandonment. What's the difference. They go. They stay. You know, and you know you know, how to fill their needs. Learn how to fill your own and have them filled. Now get off your ass and get to work! Love,
X

3/22/95

Dear Donna.

I spent the last three months in very deep introspection, while holding you in total high esteem. For the most part, you deserve to be placed there. I cut out my friends who would have me focus on you, simply because that would take the focus off me. It was necessary to insure I was not imposing my limitations on you. At the time, I didn't realize it would remove them from me. I am done with me for now, and it is time to take a look at you. I'm shaking as I write, because this is tough for me.

First let me say you are still the most powerful, phenomenal woman I have ever known. To list all your wonderful qualities would take - well, . . . go back over the last 50,000 plus words and you will get the idea. I won't take back one of them. As I possessed many flawed wonderful qualities, so do you.

On our last Wednesday together, you experienced the most powerful sexual orgasm in your life. At the end of our four hours of love making you came into full awareness of your sexual power and had the freedom through me to express it. Another explanation for this powerful orgasm is my betrayal had been arranged earlier by you. Knowing you would be free of our relationship, you were free to let go all inhibitions and self imposed restrictions. Twenty-four hours later, while you were still walking funny from me, you were having dinner with George, "and the girls."

When you finally called at 10, I felt a stab of betrayal. I swallowed my pain in both my unworthiness and my happiness for the acceptance you told me you were receiving. The acceptance I gave you was multiplying. Then, you told me about accepting a date with George, "and the girls" to go to the party the next night, our night. Another betrayal dagger in my heart. Again, I swallowed my growing pain and again subordinated my needs to yours. I knew then what was going to happen, but not for the reasons we discussed. The next day before the party, you told me you were served with divorce papers, and I knew again your vulnerability would justify your behavior.

I knew what you would be going through with the divorce. It was actually worse that I thought it would be. I knew you would need reams of support, so it was easy to put my needs aside for you. On the other hand, I also knew I did not have "all" of you. It was like about 90%. Let me tell you, 90% of you was 100 times more than I had ever received from anybody! Perhaps I have opened myself to the point where I can now feel it more clearly. You gave what you had so freely. It ran like a marlin on free spool. The line was limited by you.

All along, you kept me apprised of your increasing betrayals of the love and trust I had placed in you, and blithely ignored the fact they were betrayals. I called it what it was. You have never seen it that way, or at least admitted it to me, perhaps even to yourself. It is as though the word "betrayal" is non-existent in your vocabulary as it relates to your behavior. When you act without regard for the feelings of others, especially those who have done you no wrong, this behavior is called sociopathic. This does place you in a box. A nasty box labeled, "Sociopathic Emotional Predator." You are so much more than this yet, in personal intimate relationships, this seems to be the ultimate controlling factor.

I knew two years ago we were committing emotional adultery. You expressed concern that you didn't want to. I justified it away. We could go back and forth on it all day; the fact remains I was instrumental in your emotional betrayal of Ralph. (What goes around, comes around.) I loved you: honored, respected, accepted, validated and strengthened you. For the first time, I held a relationship consciously sacred. You showed me the power I had in doing these things. You betrayed me and conveniently turned me over to God for safekeeping. (Believe me, I'm currently in better hands!)

You are now with George, poor bastard. When your goals of financial independence and freedom (or what ever they are) are met with him, as your apparent goals of sexual freedom and increased emotional strength were met with me; with whom will you betray him next Christmas? Who will you hook next? Donna, it is not a question of "if," it is only a which Christmas and who. We both know George is too anal for you to live with, and he is hooked as surely as I was.

Honey, remember you told me that your High School counselor referred to you as one of the "coldest and hardest girls they ever came in contact with?" Way down deep, beneath your spiritual walk, you still are. It is as though God's love flows through you over this deeply imbedded soul rock, creating a maelstrom of destruction in its wake. I am so sorry for you. I have seen so much wonderful about you, and I know you have experienced some of your own inner beauty and true magnificence with me. I know you love me, because you did let me go. I hope someday you can let go of this wound to your soul as you helped me let go of the wound to mine.

I loved all of you then. I love all of you now, including this "Little Donna," whom you have protected all these years and who in turn has allowed you to satisfy your goals. Let's take a look at her. You told me what your Counselor said. You told me the molestation from your neighbor's boyfriend at 12, about the attempted rape at 13, then becoming your rapist's sex partner for six months until you had an orgasm, then dumping him. You told me about the Holiday Inn at 15, when you emotionlessly motionless let some stranger use you - perhaps to gain acceptance from your sister or family. Whatever happened to you to wound you so deeply, happened long before 12.

You shared "Little Donna" with me. You trusted me and loved me enough to let me know about her. Then you let me see her in the photographs I took. Today, I am honored by this. Very few ever get to know anyone this well, and you have protected her so well and so long. I am deeply touched by this extremely intimate sharing of who you are. I cannot think of a greater act of love. I hope someday you want to let her heal.

I no longer believe God directs this aspect of your life. All God wants from us is to be just and upright. Little Donna wants to satisfy your (her) needs, anyway she can, whether it be just and upright or not. This is a tender, wounded child as was I. She needs love and care, as did I. I do not blame her, I love her too. I know for her to heal, she will have to feel the same kind of pain I did. I don't blame her for staying behind the wall. We were too close, any more and she would have been lost, or had to feel the pain. You have protected each other for a long time. I don't blame you either. I quenched your thirst for love as you did mine. Even Little Donna's, from the outside. I just want you to know that it is there for both of you, maybe not through me, but there. I thank Little Donna too, for both sharing herself with me, and for loving me enough to chase me away.

Honey, your cruelty with me was a kindness in disguise. The way I was going, I had no chance of anything, including climbing to my own potential. My behavior was cyclic and self-defeating. Your cruel love set me free to move on and experience more of life's rewards. When you are ready to look at your behavior and the deep seated causes for it, you will. You may never be. I certainly cannot change it; only you can with a lot of help from God and your friends.

I certainly believe you would be even happier in the long run if you did, but what do I know. Right now, what you are doing seems to work for you and as long as it does you have no reason to change. Someday you may see it and change it and the world will be a much better place for all of us because of you. Love,
X

3/30/95

Dear Donna,

I guess I should thank you for coming over yesterday. I know you weren't feeling well with your cold. You were right. It was emotionally draining. I slept for an hour after you left. However, I am proud of myself for insisting on it and allowing me to fill a need for closure by confrontation. It's about time I took care of my needs. It was a need to surrender the last bit of hope I carried.

I spoke to Sam briefly last night, of course about you. She corrected me when I said "we" referring to you and I. I am still using it in the declarative. It will change to the subjunctive, "... were we..." then to "she and I," then to "her," then not at all. I worked for almost three years to build an us, a we. Even though you destroyed it in one night, it will take a while for me to change gears, downshift and not be boring.

You asked what I would have done in your place. Had I
been as close with God as I believe you to be and heard his voice
saying, "Get out," I would have given you a heads up. "Look
Honey, God wants me out of here. Maybe we should see others
and see not so much of each other." No way I could have said
that because I loved you too much. Had I your strength, well, . . .
perhaps. Besides, there's no way I could have imagined being
with somebody else. I'm still having a hard - or is it soft? - time
with that. At least now the idea is crossing my mind. Lastly, the
one thing I truly believe is behavior has its consequences. What
goes around comes around. No god I want to know would have
me betray the sacred love I felt for you. I hope my letting you go
with love mitigates any repercussions you might have from your
behavior. You have had enough hurt in your life.

Yesterday, I told you exactly where I was coming from,
what I believed to be the truth, allowed you your belief without
sacrificing mine and loved you all the while. You said you "were
afraid of being crushed." I wasn't crushing you. You were
becoming aware that Little Donna's coldness and hardness were
unnecessary but didn't want to let her go. She has protected you
for over 30 years. You in turn have protected her. My fears
were older and more comfortable. It took the pain of your
betrayal to drive them out. I don't know what it will take for you.

I am also proud of myself for not letting you off the hook
in my mind, while allowing you your beliefs. Either way, God
or Little Donna, it shows how much you screwed up by really
falling in love with me. Were it God, and there is another for me,
then it was a tremendous sacrifice on your part. Were it Little
Donna, she knew she would only hurt me worse in retribution
later on. The "another" you spoke of was simply a carrot for
diversion, or stating the obvious.

I take full responsibility for speaking to you as if I didn't
know you the first night you had dinner with George. I didn't
know you! The Donna I knew would not put herself in a
compromising situation with a guy that had been trying to buy
her for the last couple of years. That is a betrayal of my love for
and trust in you. She would not have accepted a date with him.
Little Donna would! Kill two birds with one stone. Get rid of
this guy that loves me so much, the limiting coldness that is me

might disappear; and get the store back. I loved that wounded child in you. I was delighted to see her healing. I hope the Teddy Bear I gave you, for that part of you, helps. Same on our chicken soup lunch for your cold.

Little Donna, as she exists, is a vestigial structure, like the Dover Guard. They were established around 1810 to watch for Napoleon's ships. England expected an invasion. In 1985, Queen E. said, "Excuse me. I don't think you are necessary any more," and disbanded them. Little Donna's strength is a wonderful part of you. I hope you nourish her strength as I would, gently removing her fears by action. Her directions for your behavior are, as the Dover Guard, no longer necessary. You are a phenomenal woman without this. With it . . .well, I hope your new store is extremely successful. You paid one hell of a price for it!

Anyway, I'm glad it's done. I'm sad it's done. The sadness will diminish and the gladness will remain. The memories of your love, the lessons of our love, the ecstasy of my love all shall be a treasured part of me. Should there ever be another, rest assured she will have exactly the same from me for who she is, not who I thought you were. Doing what I did with you was too wonderful for me to set aside. One difference. My needs will be met as they arise and as I meet hers. She will have to be available to meet my needs, not as you, one to whom I subordinated my needs for a future return while waiting on your full availability.

I truly hope this frees you to get on with your life as it has mine, and removes from you a barrier to your wellness. Go with God.

Love,

X

DIFFERENT SWITCH

A different switch her conscience knows
Not like yours or mine
Sometimes pushed by the hand of God
Others by the child inside

Thrice I heard of the wounded child
Twice I heard of her act
Once I saw her hardened face
I believed not the fact.

It's hard to know which is which
Or what one should expect
A radiant beauty of God's own love
Or life left in a wreck?

Her little child with wound so deep
So hard and cold and tough.
So well protected with beauty's shine
Too late we say, "enough."

Mr. X

EPILOGUE

CLEAN AND SHINY

Clean and shiny inside
as were I an old pot
long years soaking in
dirty dish water
with bits and globs
of unknown filth
matrix trapped.
(Anything strange,
unknown is filth.)

Then, lifted,
scalded, scoured,
soap scrubbed and polished
even nicks and crannies
by hand, finger
one small circle at a time
until the old pot gleams ready
providing nourishment
for those who
would eat from him.

Clean and shiny inside

8/11/95.

Lightning Source UK Ltd.
Milton Keynes UK
UKHW012202010822
406685UK00002B/270